DUNLEAVY

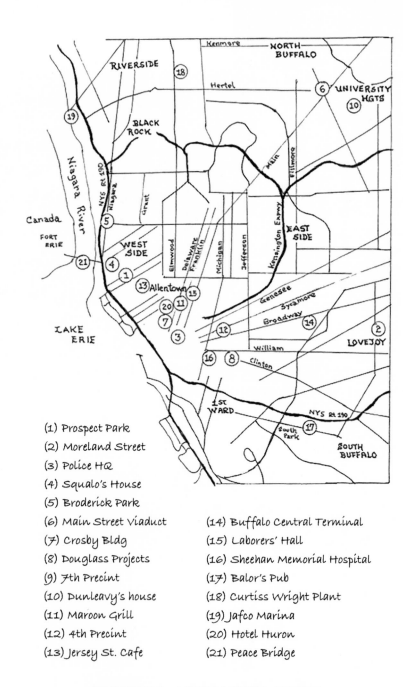

(1) Prospect Park
(2) Moreland Street
(3) Police HQ
(4) Squalo's House
(5) Broderick Park
(6) Main Street Viaduct
(7) Crosby Bldg
(8) Douglass Projects
(9) 7th Precinct
(10) Dunleavy's house
(11) Maroon Grill
(12) 4th Precinct
(13) Jersey St. Cafe

(14) Buffalo Central Terminal
(15) Laborers' Hall
(16) Sheehan Memorial Hospital
(17) Balor's Pub
(18) Curtiss Wright Plant
(19) Jafco Marina
(20) Hotel Huron
(21) Peace Bridge

BUFFALO, NEW YORK (1980)

DUNLEAVY

MARK HANNON

Encircle Publications
Farmington, Maine, U.S.A.

Encircle editor: Cynthia Brackett-Vincent

Cover design: Christopher Wait
Cover images © Getty Images

Published by:

Encircle Publications
PO Box 187
Farmington, ME 04938

info@encirclepub.com
http://encirclepub.com

To John and Marian, who got me started.

"Hell is empty and the devils are all here."
—William Shakespeare, *The Tempest*

1.

BUSTI AVENUE, THE WEST SIDE, 1979

Twitch slouched down in the Buick's crushed velvet seat and studied the house at the end of the block. He had paid attention at Squalo's cookout and watched the old people who lived behind Squalo's house finish their drinks on their back porch and turn off all the lights around 9:00. Checking his watch, he read 11:15. He quietly opened the car door and took out a big shopping bag. The paper crinkled as he grasped it, and the muscles on the left side of his neck contracted, pulling his shoulder up. *Stop,* he thought, *I must do this now for Mr. T.*

Twitch looked around but didn't see anyone. The only sound came from the wind blowing through the leaves on the maples that lined the residential street of two-story wooden houses. He moved down the block silently and slipped down the old people's driveway, noting that all the lights were off in their house. He paused by their garage and saw that the 50-foot lengths of both their backyard and Squalo's were dark. Crossing the old folks' yard, he froze for a moment when he heard mourning doves start flapping their wings up in the locust tree at the back of the property. He took a breath, then went over the low chain link fence into Squalo's yard on Columbus Parkway. He looked around once more, then went under the porch to the basement door. Putting down the shopping bag, he took out a screwdriver and checked the door handle. *Unlocked. Squalo must figure no one would dare fuck with his house.* He closed the door slowly behind him and looked around the basement with a penlight. *The shelves under the stairway. Perfect.*

Twitch found a box half filled with Christmas decorations on one of the shelves next to the gas meter. He took out the strings of lights, placed them on the floor, then pulled out a few sticks of dynamite from the grocery bag, sticking blasting caps in four of them and stacking twenty more of the red tubes in the empty box. *No more Christmases for you, you bastard.* He attached a yellow and black striped wire to a protruding filament on one of the silver blasting caps and attached the other end to a terminal on a six-volt battery, then ran another wire from the battery to a screw inserted at the seven on the exposed face of a Baby Ben alarm clock. He checked his watch, 11:30, and saw that the only hand on the ticking clock, the short hand, was pointing at eleven as he gently wiped the hand off where he had removed the finish. He then ran another black and yellow striped detonation cord from the metal clock back to the other exposed filament on the blasting cap and took a deep breath as he checked all the connections. *He'll be back from the card game by seven and asleep,* he thought as he gingerly replaced the Christmas lights on top of the bomb and crept out of the basement, his speeding pulse throbbing in his ears as he made his way back to the Buick.

Driving up the Thruway along the river towards Niagara Falls, the contractions in his neck eased, and Twitch exhaled when he drove by Mr. T's house on the quiet street of yellow brick ranch houses. "Don't worry, boss, I'm taking care of it," he whispered as he pulled into his own driveway down the block. He remembered the cookout, words spoken quietly in the kitchen when Twitch had stopped on the back stairs coming from the bathroom. Besides

Squalo, he couldn't tell who else was in the kitchen, but there was more than one.

"The old man has lost it. I brought in the take from the joints on Pine Avenue, see, and he goes and stuffs it all under a cushion on the living room couch. Doesn't count it, nothing. A couple of hours later, I get a call, and the old fool tells me to bring him his money. We gotta move now against Strazzo and his 'necktie boys' to make sure we're in charge when the boss checks out."

Twitch heard another voice that sounded like Squalo's cousin, Enzo. "What about Twitch?"

"Twitch?" Squalo said. "He can take care of the Old Man, but he's gotta stay outta the way or he's gone, the goofy spastic."

Ralph "Squalo" D'Uccisore went into his house by the side door and let out a sigh. *A good night, a* damn *good night*, he thought, as he flipped a wad of money onto the dining room table. *A lot of cash the ex'll never see, the bitch. She'll be sorry when I'm the man, and with the dope connection getting worked up, I might be as big as Genovese or the other dons in New York ever were with the frogs,* he thought. He hiked up his pants, poured himself a V.O. on the rocks, and went into the living room. Looking out the front picture window, he saw the sun just coming up over his neighborhood. He rattled the ice in the glass and turned to get another splash of whiskey.

Leo Dunleavy pulled up half a block from the scene. Hose and fire trucks were everywhere, and the firemen were hauling burned furniture out of the house and wetting it down. The middle-aged policeman parked his car well out of the way and carefully approached, noticing dollar bills fluttering around the scene as he stepped around firemen hauling ladders and dragging hose back to the red trucks with the flashing lights.

Dunleavy saw three men standing in the front yard. One was in a white shirt, wearing a helmet with a shield that read "Battalion Chief." The second was in fireman's boots and navy-blue coveralls that read "BPD-Arson" on the back. The third man was soaking wet, in a navy-blue uniform with Captain's bars on his collar. His crumpled leather helmet and rubber coat were piled next to him, and he took long pulls from a big plastic cup as he spoke. As he got close, Dunleavy could see his mustachioed face was flushed and smeared with dirt, his dark hair tangled, and he was pointing to a spot in the front yard.

"That's where we found him," the captain said. "Clothes in shreds, cut to shit, and bleeding. Said he was having a drink in his living room and *boom*—out through the picture window and into the yard. Kept asking, 'Where's my money?' Place took off after the explosion, gutted the basement and most of the first floor before we could knock it down."

The men sniffed the rank air.

"What?" the arson policeman said.

"The bomb explodes, the gas lines go and start the fire," the Battalion Chief responded. The captain snorted out a volume of sooty phlegm, nodded in agreement, and took another pull at his drink. They all looked at the man with the graying crew cut and tan sport coat who stood next to them.

The arson investigator smiled and said, "Good morning, Chief. Gentlemen, this is Lieutenant Leo Dunleavy, Chief of the Homicide Squad," and they shook hands all around. "What brings you out on a Sunday, Chief?"

"The address, Pete. Do you know whose house this is?" They all shook their heads.

"This is Ralph D'Uccisore's house," Dunleavy said.

"Squalo D'Uccisore?" the Battalion Chief asked.

"The same. Is he gonna make it?"

"Yeah, but he'll never look the same," the Captain said, and they all laughed.

Dunleavy nodded, then looked directly at the arson investigator. "Better notify the Feds, Pete. There's going to be a lot more explosions coming."

2.

THE WEST SIDE, 1979

"I'll leave this scene to you men." Dunleavy shook hands and walked back towards his car. He smiled as he overheard, "I wonder what's up," and "It's gotta be big if he's checking it out," as he got into the faded black Dodge. "Homicide 270 leaving the scene, going back to the office," he said on the radio.

"Homicide 270," the dispatcher answered, also wondering what the Chief was doing out on an early Sunday morning. Turning east on Porter, Dunleavy checked his watch. *Just 8:35, plenty of time,* he thought as he pulled into the Wilson Farms store parking lot. He exited the car and looked at the two teenagers smoking cigarettes by the front door. Not enjoying his stare, they crushed out their smokes and left the parking lot. Dunleavy nodded and went to the metal pay phone, wiping the receiver off with a cotton handkerchief. He dialed the number and smiled when it was answered on the second ring with Adele's "Hello."

"Hello, dear," he answered. "A little excitement on the West Side this morning. I'm sure you'll hear about it on the news. No, none of the boys are hurt, just one bad guy on the way to the hospital. I'll stop by the office for a while, but I'll be home in plenty of time to make the 10:30. Yes. I heard Jimmy come in last night around twelve. He may have been walking a little crooked down the hallway. Yes, I'll talk to him after Mass. Just make sure he's up and dressed. Bridget's still over at the Kazmerzak's? Yes, I heard Ceelee come home early. OK, I'll see you then. Goodbye, dear."

After all these years, he thought. Adele still wanted to be reassured of his safety when he suddenly went out. He looked around the street and, not seeing the two youths anywhere, got into the car and drove back to the yellow brick headquarters building on Franklin Street, parking in the spot marked *Chief-Homicide*.

When Dunleavy got to his office on the 4th floor, he tossed his brown snap brim fedora onto the top of the coat rack and hung up his sport coat. He took his keys out of his pocket and unlocked the file drawer with no tag in the slot. Opening it, he pulled out a frayed file from the back marked, "Lovejoy."

Sitting at his desk, he thought, *He'll come out for this one. He'll get involved, and this time I'll nail the son of a bitch.* Dunleavy flipped open the file and looked at the first item, a faded newspaper article from 1953. "Cops Baffled by Caz Creek Murder," by Robert Bray. "Buffalo Police today admitted they had few clues as to the homicide of an East Side man found Wednesday morning along Cazenovia Creek near Melrose in South Buffalo. Stepan Tovsenko, 32, of Woeppel Street was found dead by Patrolman Leo Dunleavy of the South Park Station early Thursday morning, shot 'by person or persons' unknown,' Homicide Squad Commander Lt. Pasquale Tedesco told this reporter yesterday..."

My first murder case, Dunleavy reflected. That got him hooked up with Constantino, Brogan, and Wachter for the pinball investigation. Twenty-six years ago, and the bastard's still out there, somewhere, ready to kill for the old Don, or maybe someone else now. After they didn't arrest any suspects in the Tovsenko case, he remembered saying, "What happens now? Do we just give up?" to Inspector Wachter.

Wachter told him, "Sometimes, we don't even get all the murderers, young patrolman... the trail goes cold. But, you keep your ear to the ground, and eventually, somebody in a jail cell or a bar says something to somebody, and if you're paying attention and know which doors to knock on, things open up again."

He carefully turned through the newspaper articles and yellowing typed reports, reciting what he knew about the mysterious killer no one could ever find, much less convict. Bodies found in the snow, but no footprints. Drownings in the lake ruled accidental. Missing persons never found. All of them people the Don wanted gone. Now the Feds are working to roll up the whole outfit with wiretaps and surveillance, but they don't even know this guy exists. We shook the walls interrogating the Don's boys, but none of them ever mentioned him.

Except once. They'd raided a bookmaking operation in an attic over on Garner Avenue, rounded up half a dozen of T's guys. Dunleavy was coming down the corridor where they had the suspects lined up and stopped when he heard Twitch slap the bookie and say, "Don't say a fuckin' word about Lovejoy, you idiot!" *Dammit, they should've separated them before they were booked. We might've got a line on him then,* he thought, looking at the report.

The old timers knew how to do it. Once they had one of these lowlifes in their sights, they'd get him. If they didn't get him for one thing, they'd get him for something else. They'd get his partners and squeeze them until they gave him up. I'll get him this time.

Dunleavy closed the file cabinet and drove home, parking the car in the driveway of their two-story wooden house, freshly painted blue with white trim. *The boy and I did a nice job, a nice job indeed,* he thought. As he came into the hallway, he heard the refrigerator door open in the kitchen and a pop bottle being opened. He stopped and listened to his wife talking to his son Jimmy.

"James Joseph Dunleavy. Hmmm, Pepsi in the morning? Trying to put the fire out? Yes, we heard you come in last night. You came upstairs on both sides of the stairway, I know that. Well, your father wants to talk to you after Mass. Hurry now, Dad's home, and it's time to get to church."

"All right, everybody ready to go?" Dunleavy said, and Jimmy took a large swig of soothing cola and returned it to the refrigerator. At the church, the children led the way into the pew, Cecile, the college girl with the long brown hair, and Jimmy, the high school junior. Then Adele and Dunleavy, who put the brim of his hat under the spring-loaded hook on the pew. Throughout the Mass, Dunleavy occasionally glanced over at Jimmy, who was having a hard time keeping his eyes open. Adele frowned and nudged him from time to time, while Cecile and Dunleavy smiled.

Back at the house, Dunleavy tapped his boy on the shoulder and waved him into the den. The boy followed, eyes downcast. When they were both seated, Dunleavy cleared his throat and said, "Jimmy, you and your friends were drinking last night, and when you came home, you were bouncing off the walls."

The boy nodded.

"Now, I'm not about to tell you I didn't tip a few at your age. Hell, I had my first beer when I was fourteen," he said, his voice rising. "You're grounded for two weeks, son. No dances, no basketball games. You come home from school, do your homework, and stay home. Got it?"

Jimmy nodded and started to get up. Dunleavy touched him on the sleeve and he sat down again.

"Another thing," he said, emphasizing the lesson with his index finger pointing at the boy's nose. "Never, *ever* get in a car, and especially, don't drive after you boys have cracked that first beer, or I'll box your ears. Do you understand?"

Jimmy's head receded and his eyes crossed slightly as his dad's blue eyes focused on his and the finger pointed like a pistol. He was almost as tall as his father now, just under the elder's 5'11," but was outweighed by thirty pounds. Thinking of his father's promise to box his ears, he remembered a time at a Bills game in Rich Stadium when Cecile was coming back from the concession stand with hot dogs for them, and some young drunk grabbed her butt as she went by. His dad saw it, stood up, put his hat on his chair, walked down to where the youth sat with his friends, hauled the guy up from his seat, and knocked him down the steps. The guy's nose bloodied, he jumped up and started shouting and waving his hands. His dad stood his ground, and the guy and his friends shouted obscenities and threats but kept their distance. When the security guards showed up, his dad went over to one he knew, a sheriff's deputy. They spoke for a few moments while the guy kept screaming, then the deputy waved to the other security guards, who grabbed the drunk and dragged him out of the stadium.

"OK, Dad, I promise. I'll be careful."

Dunleavy patted the teenager on the shoulder and nodded.

"I know you will, son. Now go out in the kitchen and see what your mother has fixed us for lunch. I'll be right down after I change."

Adele overheard the conversation in the den from the pantry and nodded in approval while she sliced up roast beef for sandwiches. She heard Dunleavy go up the stairs, waited until he hung his sport coat in the closet, then shouted, "Put your shirt down the laundry shoot."

"I only wore it for a couple of hours," he replied, the shirt in one hand and a hanger in the other.

"We've got plenty of clean shirts!" she shouted, thinking, *he still thinks his mother has to wash all the clothes in the old tub wringer.*

3.

F.B.I. SGO SQUAD OFFICE, AMHERST, NY, 1979

F.B.I. Special Agent Kevin Shea sat at his government-issued steel desk in the industrial park warehouse, waiting for two of his street agents to return. He'd left the house at 5 a.m., dressing in the dark to not wake the wife, and left a note on the kitchen table saying he'd be back by lunchtime so she wouldn't call the office in the federal building looking for him. Better if the office pogues downtown didn't know what his squad was doing sometimes.

He heard about the bombing and fire at Squalo's house and, scratching the red curls on his head, wondered who'd done it. Probably Strazzo, but a bomb wasn't his style. Too loud and attracted too much attention. The old Don wouldn't do it that way, and that's how Strazzo operated, too. It might be somebody helping Strazzo from out of town, or one of the Don's family that didn't like Squalo. No witnesses so far. Squalo was in the hospital, and the explosives could've been from almost any construction company in the area. Well, if Silverstein and Amodeo got the bugs in right, they should be hearing intercepts from the Jersey Street Café about who did what shortly. Shea chuckled to himself, thinking he was made the case agent on this operation because he was one of the few in the office with the patience to write a seventy-six-page affidavit request to infiltrate the café. That "T-III Affidavit" had then traveled up the chain of command in Buffalo, then onto headquarters in Washington and the Department of Justice, and finally back after weeks of review for him and an Assistant U.S. Attorney to take it to the judge for the court order. Hell, at this pace, they might all be retired before anything happens and this war on the West Side is over.

The phone rang, and Shea looked at his watch. *0710, they should be done by now, they should be back here.*

"Special Agent Shea."

"Mr. Shea, this is Frances Schuppe, the night clerk downtown. I have a phone call for you from Lt. MacIntyre of the Buffalo Police Department. Should I put him through?"

Shea looked up from his desk as Amodeo and Silverstein came in, dressed in dark turtlenecks and workout pants. He waved them over as he said, "Yes, Frances, put him on... Well, Mac, you're up early. What's going on?"

"You're up bright and early as well for a Sunday, Kevin. I was calling to give you an update on the bombing over on Columbus Parkway."

"Good, good, Keith," he said as Amodeo and Silverstein stood in front of his desk smiling. "What have you got for me?" he said as Amodeo gave him a thumbs up.

"Not much at this point, to tell you the truth. The bomber must have used about twenty sticks of dynamite, initiated the explosion with blasting caps set off by a battery wired to an alarm clock— we found bits of spring and gears from the clock lodged in the wood of the floorboards. D'Uccisore was lucky—he was standing by the picture window in front of his house. The blast blew him out into the front yard. Cut him all to hell, but he's going to live. It also ripped out the gas pipes and set the place on fire, which isn't making it any easier to investigate."

"Any witnesses?"

"Not so far."

"D'Uccisore say anything yet?"

"No, but you didn't expect him to, did you? His biggest concern was the money that was blowing all over the street, and he's not saying where that came from either."

Shea paused and looked at the chart on the wall, showing a flow chart of the Buffalo Mafia. At the top was written in large black letters "BUFFALO L.C.N." and under that, an old picture from the fifties showing a bald, bullet-headed man with no neck, smiling in a dark suit. Under the photograph it read "Vincente Tutulomundo, aka. Mr. T/Boss/Commission Member." Off to the side, there was a picture of Torreo Monteduro from the same era, and under him, it read "Consiglieri (retired-Florida)." Directly beneath Tutulomundo were two names, "Ralph (Squalo) D'Uccisore/Underboss" and next to him, "Grant (Strazzo) Strozzare/Underboss," both pictured in fairly recent mugshots. D'Uccisore, with bulging dark eyes, bushy hair, and thick lips, wore an open-collar shirt. Strozzare wore a suit, his chin was tilted up, his silver hair parted on the side, and he had slits for eyes that made him look like he was staring through smoke.

"Well, thanks, Keith. You think there's a war starting?"

"Strazzo and Squalo both want to be the man next, Kevin, and from what we hear, T's too far out of it to control them. Chief Dunleavy figures all hell's about to break loose and thought we should pass the information on to you."

Dunleavy, Shea thought. *That guy reads a crime scene like Stabler reads defenses.* "Well, thanks again, Keith, for telling us what you have so far. Let us know what else you turn up, OK?"

"Sure, Kev, and we hope you'll let us know whatever you guys hear out there in Amherst."

Huh, Shea thought. *He's fishing for information we get off the wiretaps.* And with that, he hung up.

"Well, boys," he said, rubbing his hands together, "are we ready to listen into the ongoing adventures of Squalo and company?"

"The back room and the upstairs are both rigged..." Amodeo said.

"Activated and transmitting," added Silverstein.

"Well," Shea said, getting up from his desk, "let's get the recorders up and running, gentlemen. According to Lt. Dunleavy and others of the Buffalo Police, there appear to be war clouds gathering on Buffalo's West Side."

4.

JERSEY STREET CAFÉ, THE WEST SIDE, 1934

Vincente Tutulomundo was feeling expansive that warm summer day. By the time he had finished his first cup of coffee, three of his men had dropped off their take. It was easier now, since that *manga patat* cop Mulhern had finally retired. When that damned Mick was around, he used to tell the waiter to leave a broom outside propped up against the storefront, so his men would know the place was being watched and to bring the money to Monteduro.

The breeze was blowing through the screen door of the café, and T waved the waiter off for the second cup. He got up, put on his white cap, and walked down to Niagara, nodding to those who greeted him and checking how business was in the shops—if they were doing better than expected, he wanted to adjust the tribute accordingly, depression or not.

He crossed Porter after carefully looking up and down the street. Two years ago, there were some foolish men who tried to ambush him here. They fired several pistol shots at him from a car, hitting Piazza. He and Monteduro fired back, shattering the windshield and the radiator. They took Piazza to the pharmacist's house on Busti, then asked around the neighborhood to identify the gunmen riding around in the damaged car. A month later, one of them was found on fire, hanging from a tree right where the shooting took place, and the other was never found at all.

Crossing over into Prospect Park, T saw some boys playing a game. They were lined up in two lines with interlocking arms, facing each other. One line shouted, "Red Rover, Red Rover, send Tommy over!" and braced themselves. A boy from the other line charged them, his legs jerking awkwardly. He bounced off his opponent's line but grabbed onto one boy's outstretched arm and tried to pull himself through. When that didn't work, Tommy bit the boy's arm, and when he pulled his arm away, threw himself through the line. All the boys started yelling.

"Cheater!"

"That doesn't count! He bit him!"

The boy who was bit started swinging his fists at Tommy and knocked him down. Tommy kicked at him and tried to drag him down but got the worst of it as the other boys gathered around to watch and shout.

"Bust him up, Frankie!"

"Hit that spaz-bunny! Hit him, Frankie!"

A man reading a newspaper on a bench got up, pushed his way through the boys and separated Tommy and Frankie as T watched. The boys scattered, but Tommy kept trying to attack Frankie as the man held them apart. Finally, Tommy gave up and lurched off in T's direction.

"You lose, huh?" T asked him.

"I'll get 'em," Tommy said, wiping the blood from his face.

Two days later, T had just put a few drops of cold water into his anisette at a table outside the bar on Vermont when Tommy went past him into the tavern carrying a growler. While he was in there, Frankie and another kid came by and stopped to admire the blue Chevrolet Master Coupe that had pulled up out front. Carrying the full growler, Tommy came out the tavern door and he spotted his adversary. He hesitated a moment, then pitched the beer at

Frankie and started swinging the empty pail onto Frankie's head. The men at the tables pulled them apart and were shoving the boys off when T beckoned Tommy over.

"You're still mad at him, yes?" T said, pointing with his chin at the retreating Frankie.

"He's a shit."

"You lose the beer now, too."

"I don't care, I got 'em back."

"Whose beer?"

Tommy's right shoulder jerked up to his neck, and he shook his head.

T slapped him. "I said, whose beer, twitch boy?"

Tommy looked down but said nothing. One of the other men said in Italian, "Probably his mother's. She and her friends play cards on Saturdays and drink out on the back porch all day, until they go to work at night." The other men laughed.

T spoke in Italian, "Where is the father?"

The other man shrugged. T looked at the boy and handed him a quarter.

"Get more beer," T commanded, and as Tommy took the coin, T added, "You want to make money?"

Twitch nodded.

"Come to the Jersey Street Café tomorrow morning. You will run errands."

5.

THE WEST SIDE, 1934

After a few weeks of running errands successfully, T called Twitch aside at his table in the café.

"You know what it means when the waiter puts a broom outside?"

"It means the police are around."

"And when Strazzo, Squalo and the others come and bring me things?"

"They're delivering the money."

"Do you know who the policemen are?"

Twitch nodded. "Yes, there's four of them who come around here. The plainclothesmen they call them. They change sometimes, but everyone gets quiet or leaves when they're around."

"Good. Sometimes I will have you watching. Sometimes from upstairs, sometimes from the corners, sometimes from other places. You will watch and let us know if the police are coming," and with that, he gave Twitch a dime. "Now, go get some ice cream… and remember," he said, touching the knuckle of his index finger to his lips.

Twitch nodded and said, "Say nothing" as he skipped off with the dime.

6.

JERSEY STREET CAFÉ, THE WEST SIDE, 1942

Squalo and Strazzo were sitting at the boss' table in the café reading the paper, and Twitch was leaning against the wall watching the street when T came in. Both men started to get up until T gently waved his fingers for them to remain seated. Sitting down and fanning himself with his white cap, T tapped his index finger on the newspaper and asked, "So, this war goes on. Is the army going to take you two?"

Both men shrugged.

"This rationing, it makes coffee, sugar, meat, gasoline, hard to get, yes?"

Strazzo whispered, "The gasoline comes up the coast by ship from Texas and travels west to Buffalo by tanker truck."

Squalo leaned forward. "Our drivers see the gasoline tanker men every morning getting coffee in Beachy's on Route 20. Very quiet out there."

"We have room in our garages to keep such trucks until we empty them?"

Both underlings nodded. Squalo added, "I've been talking to a bunch of filling stations around. They'll take as much as we can get them."

T tapped his hand twice on the table, and Strazzo and Squalo got up and left. When T left, Twitch got the phone book out and found "Office of Price Administration, Crosby Building, Bflo."

1.

DARIEN CENTER, NY, 1942

Squalo got up from the shaky wooden table and followed the green uniformed driver to the back lot of the diner, where his cousin Enzo was sitting on the tanker truck's running board.

"No riders, buddy," the driver in the uniform cap said, pointing to the sign painted on the cab door. Enzo smiled at him, stood up, and hefted a foot-long piece of pipe.

From behind, Squalo said, "He likes the dinosaur," referring to the green figure painted on the cylindrical trailer.

The driver spun around to see the six-foot Squalo with his fists clenched at his side.

"Wha—what's going on here?" the wide-eyed driver yelled.

"I've got twenty bucks says you want some pie and another cup of coffee," Squalo said. "When you're finished, the truck is gone and you don't know nothing."

The driver looked back at Enzo, who was tapping the pipe in his open palm.

"Your choice, my friend," Squalo said.

"Yeah, yeah, OK," the driver said.

"The keys," Squalo demanded.

Squalo exchanged the twenty for the keys and looked at the driver's sewn name tag. "Say nothing… Paul. We can find you."

It was just before dawn when they pulled into the warehouse.

"All right," Squalo said. "Now you get on the phone and call those gas stations. We want to move this stuff as fast as possible and get rid of the truck before the cops start looking for it."

"Gotcha," Enzo said, and headed for the office.

A truck's horn sounded out behind the warehouse, paused, then blew again, longer. Squalo walked out there and saw an Esso tanker truck idling at the warehouse's back door. Strazzo was sitting in the passenger's seat and his friend Robby, the bus driver, behind the wheel. Strazzo rolled the window down as Squalo approached.

"Open the door, Ralph, we gotta get this rig outta sight before the sun comes up."

"No can do, Strazzo. We got another truck in here now."

"What the hell, I gotta get this baby off the street before sunup, the cops'll be looking for it."

Squalo noticed blood on Strazzo's jacket.

"What the hell happened?" Squalo said, pointing at the blood.

"Son of a bitch gave me an argument. Turns out he owned the truck."

"Take the damn thing over to Maish's over on Tonawanda. This place is occupied."

"You S.O.B.! I gotta have this space!"

Squalo waved him off and went back inside, slamming the door.

"You no good bastard! All right goddammit! Let's get this truck up the street to Maish's, Robby. I'll deal with that *stronzo* later."

As the tanker drove north up Niagara Street, Captain Martin Wachter was coming down Niagara, sitting next to his driver Tom Keating. He had just checked that the units patrolling the northern end of his precinct were doing exactly that and was on his way back for the a.m. roll call when the tanker truck approached, the driver revving the engine twice before he got it to drop into third gear.

"Dummy can't handle that clutch right," Keating said.

Wachter looked up and saw the oft-arrested Strazzo in the cab.

"Hit the siren, Tom, those guys are up to no good."

When Wachter spotted the blood on Strazzo's jacket, he drew his revolver and had Keating handcuff the two men in the middle of Niagara Street, where Strazzo's neighbors could see it. As the policeman shoved them into the patrol car, he heard Strazzo muttering obscenities in Italian and something about... *quel bastardo Squalo.*

8.

DOWNTOWN BUFFALO, 1942

Twitch pulled a crowbar and a rubber mallet out from under his jacket when he descended the steps to the basement door in the alley. He took a deep breath, put the special A-forked claw end on the cylinder lock and tapped it down with the mallet. He adjusted the angle of the crow bar and tapped it again until it was firmly wedged behind the cylinder. Grabbing the other end of the crow bar and using his body weight, he pulled it down until the cylinder came loose and pulled it out of the door. He examined the cylinder, inserted a thin L-shaped piece of steel into the lock, turned it and unlocked the door. Once inside, he stopped and listened for a moment, heard nothing and walked through the musty-odored basement. He stopped again to listen. *Nothing,* he thought, *and the watchman is up on the second floor in his office, just like every night, the elevator operator said.*

Turning on the flashlight, he walked over to the stairs and started to slowly climb, shutting off the flashlight at the second floor. He stopped there and listened, hearing the watchman's radio playing and the guard singing "I've Got a Gal... in Kalamazoo." He crept up to the fourth floor, walked down the hallway to where the O.P.A. office was, and jimmied the door with the flathead screwdriver. Once inside, he went past the desks in the outer office, used the screwdriver again on the director's door and went to the big green cabinet behind the desk he had spotted the week before when asking a clerk for a leather cover for his ration book. *Cheap government issued cabinet,* he thought as he pulled out the crowbar. *Now, this is the risky part.* He placed the sharpened flat edge of the crowbar in the narrow space between the wide cabinet doors and pried until he had a purchase next to the lock, then reinserted the crowbar deeper and pried again until the doors popped open, quivering noisily. He stopped and listened again. Still nothing. He pulled out the flashlight and started looking through the middle shelves where he'd first spotted them.

There they are, he thought as he scooped up the sheets of gasoline ration stickers and put them in the paper grocery bag. Exiting the office, he shut the doors behind him. While going down the stairs past the third floor, he heard the watchman clear his throat and jangle his keys. He scampered down the steps past the second floor just as the guard came into the stairwell, and that's when the crowbar slipped out from his jacket and clanged on the cast iron steps.

"Who the hell is that?" the guard said, playing his oversized lantern down towards Twitch. Twitch ran down the steps to the basement and outside into the greasy airshaft, the guard still thumping down the stairway two floors behind him. He wrapped up the paper bag as tight as he could and stashed it in a trash can behind the building. As he ran down the cobblestone alley, he heard the guard yell, "Stop! Thief! Police!" and then he heard policemen's whistles start going off from several directions.

Twitch waited in the cell, tapping his foot and trying to control the tremors. *I gotta tell them where it is before they pick up the trash. When do they pick up the trash behind the Crosby Building?*

When Squalo came into bail him out, Twitch said nothing to anyone, just nodded and signed papers. He barely breathed until they got outside, where Enzo was behind the wheel of the boss's purple Cadillac. Once inside the car, both made men turned to him in the back seat.

"What? You got anything for us?" Squalo said.

"Something? Anything?" Enzo said as Twitch shook, trying to get his voice.

"There's a package… Ration coupons stashed in a paper bag in the trash… in Bean Alley… behind the Crosby Building on Franklin."

Wheels squealed as the caddy pulled off. When they got to the alley, Twitch pointed to the row of trash cans. The car screeched to a halt and the doors flew open. Squalo and Enzo started knocking over the trash cans, scattering debris all over the alley. A janitor carrying two bags of trash out of the building stopped when he saw the men's frenzy.

"Get the hell outta here, you son-of-bitch!" Squalo shouted at the janitor, and upended another of the metal ribbed canisters, reeking food waste splattering on the cobblestones. The Black man retreated back into the building.

"That one! That one's it," Twitch said, pointing at a can Enzo had in hand. He upturned it, but only office papers came out. The two hoods looked at Twitch.

"That's it, I tell you!" Twitch said. Enzo looked in the can, smiled, turned it back upside down and banged on the bottom. A folded brown paper package fell out. Enzo tossed the can aside, but Squalo beat him to the package. Looking inside, Squalo said, "This is it!" and the three of them got in the car, Twitch almost falling out as he struggled to close the suicide door as they peeled away. They wheeled around and Enzo almost crashed into a Ford waiting at the streetlight at Mohawk as he looked over to see what Squalo was examining.

"Holy shit, there's gotta be dozens of A Stickers in here," Squalo said. Twitch, hands on the seats in front of him, smiled and looked from Enzo to Squalo, waiting.

"They gotta be worth thousands on the street!" Enzo said.

"Yeah. We'll have to be careful who we sell 'em to. This many's bound to attract attention."

"We can sell 'em outta town, anywhere!"

Twitch sat back in the seat until they got to the restaurant on the Terrace, where T was having lunch in the back room. Twitch followed the other two, Squalo holding the package tightly under his arm. They waited at the entrance to the dining room until T signaled them to approach. They stood at the edge of the table, Twitch almost invisible behind the other two.

Squalo whispered, "Looks like the bail money wasn't wasted, Mr. T." After T had taken a sip of water and daubed his lips, Squalo handed him the package. He looked inside and nodded.

"Have them put this in the restaurant's safe for now," T said, pointing with his fork at the package. "I'll decide about it later."

The two bigger men turned, bumping Twitch, who staggered back a step.

"Oh," T said, and they turned back. He motioned Enzo closer with his knife.

"Find him a woman for tonight," T said, pointing with the knife to Twitch.

The girl came in the house through the unlocked driveway entrance, walked up the stairs and knocked on the door to Twitch's flat.

"Who's there?" Twitch said as he tuned the radio to the baseball game.

"Your friends sent me."

Twitch jumped. The voice sounded familiar. Almost like his mother's. He got up from the table and opened the door. She was skinny, wearing khaki slacks and a purple blouse. Dead brown eyes in a face with hastily applied lipstick stared at him. He looked down the stairs where Mrs. Ficanasso's door was ajar and she behind it.

"Do you want me to come in?" the girl said.

"Yes, yes, come on in," he said. He closed the door quietly. "Have a seat, have a seat," indicating the kitchen table with the radio on it. She put her purse down there and withdrew a pack of cigarettes.

"Uh, do you want something to drink?" he said.

She tossed back her brown curls and blew a smoke ring up towards the overhead light.

"Sure. Got any rye?" He went to a cupboard and pulled out a bottle of Imperial with two inches of whiskey left in it, then rinsed two glasses from the sink.

He watched her stand at the dresser, brushing out her brown curls with the hairbrush she pulled from her purse. There was no tension in him for the first time he could remember, from his jaw to his toes. He sat up as she shouldered her purse.

"Um, what's your name, sweetie?"

"Sonia."

"How about dinner sometime, Sonia? I know lots of good places."

"Sure," she said, pulling a pencil from her purse. As she wrote her number down, she said, "Your friends got me a phone, here's the number. I work the three to eleven shift at Trico, so call early. It's five bucks from now on, not including dinner."

9.

THE WEST SIDE, 1942

Twitch started calling Sonia weekly, trying to catch her early in the morning before she went to work. When he was very excited, he'd have her come right over to his house. Other times, he'd take her out to the movies or dinner first.

"Hey, I see *Phantom Lady* is playing at Shea's Seneca."

"No, I'm not going there."

"How come? They say it's a good movie."

"I'm not going there, Twitch."

She always took the bus home after leaving his house. Once, he followed her to a house on Rutland Street in South Buffalo. He watched for a while and he figured out she lived in the upstairs flat by herself.

"How about dinner at DiTondo's?"

"I'm not going there, Twitch."

She never wanted to go with him anywhere in South Buffalo. She did like going to McVan's up on Ontario Street in Black Rock, where she'd meet him after work, or the Maroon Grill over on Pearl, where she'd pick a table in a dimly lit corner.

"How's your dinner?" he asked.

She stopped working her knife and fork on the pork chops long enough to say, "It's fine, just fine."

She was lighting up a cigarette when she spotted a brunette with an omelet fold hairdo go up to the bar.

"Hmmpf," Sonia said, flicking ashes.

Twitch turned, and spotting the woman, said, "Huh, Gene Tierney." Sonia tossed her hair. A man sidled up to the woman and whispered something.

"Get the hell away from me," the brunette said, and kicked him with her pointed shoe right under the kneecap.

"Dammit all, bitch!" the man said, grabbing his knee and hopping away. Everyone laughed, Sonia loudest of all.

When they got back to Twitch's flat, he hung up her coat.

"That was funny tonight, with the brunette."

She chuckled as she took off her brown dress.

"Yeah, it sure was," she laughed.

She's happy, he thought. *I made her laugh.*

10.

SOUTH BUFFALO, 1945

Twitch dialed Sonia's number for the third time, and for the third time, got a busy signal. He paused, then dialed the operator.

"Operator," a voice said.

"Yes, uh miss, I keep calling Fairview 3914 and keep getting busy signals."

Twitch heard a loud sigh, then, "Maybe, sir, the other party is on the phone, or if it is a party line, one of the other parties is using it."

"Uh, I know it's a private line, and I've tried all different times of the day."

"The receiver might be off the hook… sir."

"Well, can you check to see if that number's working?"

Another sigh. "Yes sir, give me your number and I'll call you back."

Twitch looked out the window, paced and fiddled with the radio. Finally, the phone rang.

"Yes?"

"This is the operator. The number you've been calling? It has been disconnected."

"That can't be. I paid for the private line, I…"

"I'm sorry sir, that number is no longer working," and the line went dead.

Twitch ran downstairs and drove over to where Sonia lived. She was out front, a driver loading luggage into a yellow cab.

"What… what's going on, Sonia?"

She closed her eyes and shook her head. "I'm getting the hell out of town. For good, Twitch."

"But… but what about you and me?"

"There is no you and me, Twitch. Find another playmate. Your friends on Jersey Street can help you."

"No!" he shouted, and the cab driver started coming towards him. Sonia waved him off and walked towards Twitch. She was wearing an orange rayon dress that just touched her knees and her hair was in a Victory Roll.

"Look, mister. I'm getting out of here. No more making bullets at Trico, no more working in the dark keeping strangers entertained, no more sharing my cash with those God damned mob friends of yours. This war's going to end soon, and I'm going to meet my husband out West when it's over."

"Wha'?"

The driver gave Twitch a hard look as he opened the passenger door for Sonia. She swung her bare legs into the cab, the door slammed shut and they left him standing in the driveway, his neck and shoulders trembling.

He remembered his mother, after he'd been working for T for about a year. He saw her getting on the Number 3 streetcar going downtown with a suitcase. When he got back to the house, there was a note on the table.

Tommy,

Now that you've got a job you can take care of yourself. I'm going away for a while. There's the leftover chicken in the icebox for dinner tonight.

He remembered opening the ice box door. Yeah, there it was, half a chicken. There was some other food in there too, but looking on the counter, he saw a bunch of empty beer bottles. From the different cigarette butts in the ashtrays, she and somebody else drank all the beer. He smelled aftershave, too. *To hell with them, to hell with them all, I don't need them, I'm with the men on Jersey Street now and forever.*

11.

LOVEJOY, THE EAST SIDE, 1946

Andy woke up when he heard the front door open and the full coal bucket clunk on the floor. His blanket was half kicked off and the room was cold. He could hear the wind rattle the loose windowpane as he sat up on the bed. The wooden floorboards chilled his feet when he stood up and walked out into the hallway where his father was trudging towards him unseeing, his heavy work shoes clomping on the creaking floor. Andy smelled the coal smoke on his father's coat as he brushed past him.

"Papa?" Andy said.

His father nodded as he pulled off his coat. "I have to sleep a few hours now," he said, "before I go back to the depot. Walk Bailey before you go to school," he said, scratching the beagle's head, then went in his room and lay down on the bed. Andy stood there for a minute, then turned away when he heard his father start to snore. *Two days shoveling coal into a train's firebox to New York and back and this is all it gets you,* Andy thought, looking around the tiny cottage.

Andy went back to his room and yanked on the ill-fitting drawer at the top of the scarred dresser and pulled out clean underwear. He got corduroy pants and a flannel shirt from the other drawer and his tie hanging off the mirror. *Dad got me this tie from Sattler's when I started high school. Cheap, out of style junk,* he thought. He gathered up the clothes and took them into the bathroom. He washed his face and ears and opened up the medicine chest to get his comb and brush out. *Not much in there now.* He remembered dad had thrown away all mom's makeup and stuff from there after she took off with the engineer from the New York Central. He brushed his hair straight back, then carefully parted it on the right side. He smiled, thinking, *That D.P. girl, Maja, likes my blonde hair. I'll get her behind the stage at the dance Saturday.*

When Andy went out in the kitchen, the beagle looked up at him from the only cushioned chair in the room. He saw the bucket of coal his father had brought back from the rail yard and thought about getting a fire going in the potbellied stove, but that would get him a whipping. He went to the single cupboard over the sink and looked inside. *There it is,* he thought, looking at the green tin box where they'd kept all their savings before mom snatched it when she left. He remembered coming home from school and finding his father in shock, sitting at the kitchen table, the battered box open and empty before him.

"All of it. Every nickel we saved to buy a house," he had kept muttering.

Andy looked in the box now. *Two nickels, a dime and three pennies. Not worth the beating I'd get to steal it for the dance,* he thought. He grabbed the box of corn flakes that was next to it, got the milk bottle from the chilly window sill and fixed himself breakfast. When he picked up his books, the dog jumped off the chair and ambled over to the door. He heard the church bells from St. Agnes ring 7:30. *All right, I've got time to walk you, you lazy bum,* he thought, and pulled the leash off the hook on the door. He put his books down and they went out of the cottage through the back yard, past the big house in front and out onto the icy sidewalk. When the dog started to squat on the sidewalk, Andy kicked the beagle over to the curb where he defecated. Finished,

Bailey trotted up the street, pausing in front of Mr. Artiano's old Ford. He lapped up something under the front of the car, and Andy yanked him along back to the sidewalk.

When Andy came home from school, the house was even colder, if that was possible, and Bailey's head was hanging off the chair. He looked at the dog, looked at the bucket of coal and took it over to the stove. He gathered some busted up sticks, bits of scrap wood and old newspaper from the freight box next to the stove, carefully selected one of the better split matches from the matchbox on the cook stove and started a fire. When the kindling was going, he carefully added a measure of coal, and when he was sure it was going, went over and picked up the dog's head. It flopped loose when he let it go. He picked up the dead animal and took it behind the house in front of their cottage where he dropped it in one of the galvanized trash cans. He went back down the driveway into the cottage where he washed his hands and started dinner for his father and himself.

12.

SHEEHAN MEMORIAL HOSPITAL, BUFFALO, 1979

After forty-eight hours, the doctors allowed the police to talk to Squalo. All his people were gone and Squalo was lying on his back, trying to focus on the goddamn cop in the hallway. *Was that fucker smiling at me? I swear to God, I'm going to get out of this bed and kick his ass. Those shots they give me are wearing off. Fuck it, I'll show them, I won't ask for them,* he thought, gritting his teeth.

The blue suited officer turned, looked down the hallway and nodded in recognition. *What the fuck now,* Squalo thought, as three guys in sports coats and mismatched ties came into the room.

"Mr. D'Uccisore, I'm Lieutenant MacIntyre of the Police Arson Squad," the first one said, holding up his badge. "And this is Detective Cappetta," he said, pointing a thumb to his right, "and Fire Investigator Fitch," pointing to his left. "We'd like to ask you some questions about the explosion and fire at your house on Columbus Parkway."

Squalo started taking deep breaths, and he noticed a fourth person in a sports coat in the room, standing behind the three detectives. *It's that goddamn Dunleavy, the homicide cop. That prick's been after me for years.* Squalo took another deep breath, and though it sent pain searing through his back and shoulders, reached over to the far bed railing and pulled himself on his side, facing away from the policemen. The hospital gown parted in the back and Squalo held himself in that position, gritting his teeth, until the policemen left.

13.

SHEEHAN MEMORIAL HOSPITAL, BUFFALO, 1979

Squalo took very small breaths as long as he could. When he took a deep one, it stretched the burned and cut skin and pain flashed in fifty places, front and back. The whole room smelled of the damned medicine they treated the wounds with, and it stung like hell as they applied it. The worst was when they rolled him over. He pushed the nurse away and swung at the medical assistant when they first tried it, and he screamed when he flopped back on his ass. Two more aides came in.

"We've got to turn you, Mr. D'Uccisore. To treat the wounds on your back and so you won't get infections there!"

After five more minutes of fighting them, Squalo was exhausted. Enzo was there and gave him an out to stop fighting them.

"Ralph, you gotta listen to these people! You gotta do what they say to heal!"

The whole damn thing had been an embarrassment from the start. He remembered the explosion, flying through the window. Rolling around on the front lawn in a daze, his clothes in shreds, watching his money float down like snowflakes. The neighbors coming out in their pajamas, looking at him, looking at the money flutter around.

"Don't... don't touch any of it. It's mine," he gasped, helpless.

Then the sirens and all those guys stomping past him with their hoses and ladders like he wasn't even there. The ambulance people, wiping him down and talking.

"Doesn't seems anything's broken, Ernie."

"No major bleeding. Let's load him and go," Ernie said.

"On two. One, two!" and they nearly dropped him as they heaved his 240 pounds onto the gurney. He faded in and out as they jabbed him with an IV in the back of the ambulance and Squalo rocked back and forth as the siren wailed through the streets to the hospital, telling the world, *Squalo is down, Squalo is hurt!*

Who? Who did this? was his constant thought. Between the drugs and the ever more painful debriding treatments, *We have to get all the dead tissue off, Mr. D'Uccisore, or it will get infected,* they said, scrubbing the raw skin with treated dressings. His mind wandered through the next hours, trying to concentrate. *Strazzo,* he thought, time and again. As his head gradually cleared and pains sharpened, he thought, *it's got to be him.* Doubts came sometime— Strazzo would do it the old way, like T, with a garrote wielded by his own men, to show he was the new T, the new boss. *The cops would be watching him though. The FBI bastards with their cameras. He'd hire somebody from outside, that's it. They'd do it their way— Cleveland! Those guys use bombs all the time, like when they blew up that Greene character a couple of years back. Who sanctioned it? Some assholes in New York? They hate that I'm dealing with the Dominicans with the dope. When I get the hell out of here I'm going to kill all of them. Start right on the West Side and work out.*

The worst part was the cop in the hallway.

"Get that fucker outta here!" he'd screamed, and Enzo jumped up from the chair by his bed. "My people! I want just my people in here!"

The aides rushed in and kept him from jumping off the bed, then gave him a shot.

"Ralph! Take it easy man! He's just out in the hallway! He's not allowed in here, don't worry!"

Squalo was flying on painkillers. In his dream, it was snowing money, but every time he tried to grab some, it slipped through his fingers. His neighbors were all there in their pajamas, trying to snatch up the money, and Strazzo was standing there, laughing at him. He smelled something. *That lime-gin smell. Hair tonic.* Starting to come to, he looked around and tried to focus. There were two people in the room at his bedside. *Strazzo! That Kreml Hair Tonic he always wore, that's what he smelled. Look at the bastard. Manicured fingernails.* Squalo wondered if he'd done any real work after being sent up for the tanker truck job. He remembered the tanker truck driver testifying, his head in bandages. *Strazzo did four years for that,* he thought.

Huh, he brought his boy Z with him, too. Looks like they both just came from the barber, Strazzo with his businessman's cut and Z with his 50's flat top. What the hell is he saying. He's got my hand in his two paws, now Z's saying something about "Be well." You phony motherfuckers, I'll get you both.

14.

THE EAST SIDE, 1979

Nate Harwood woke up on the old hospital bed and looked around the darkened room, wondering where he was. *Shit, that's right, I'm at Phyllis and Willie's house.* He twisted the switch for the lamp on the stand next to the bed. *Nothing.* He did it again and it came on, illuminating the ten by twelve-foot basement room. *I'm living in the old coal bin in the basement. Better than the joint, but what the fuck, I gotta do better than this.*

As he buttoned one of Willie's old flannel shirts, he listened to the house. He heard the dog scrambling across the wooden floor upstairs, and that was all. *Everybody's gone by this time. Willie and Phyllis are at work and the kids are at school.* He went into the open basement and then up the stairs. He checked the door that led into the kitchen and heard the dog scratching at it, remembering Phyllis asking him to walk their pet. *Later for you, dog. Yeah, Nate, you can stay with us until you get on your feet again, your convict ass can walk the dog when we're not around.*

He turned on the landing and left the house through the back door. He walked out on the street and his feet took him off the residential street up to Jefferson where there might be something happening. He looked at the hand painted sign on the store. Community Seafood, yeah, somebody might be hanging there, he thought, ambling towards it. Inside, the smell of fresh fish filled his nostrils and the fillets laid out on ice again reminded him it was better than Attica.

"Well, goddamn, if it ain't Nate Harwood!" the man in the broad brimmed hat said.

Nate looked up and spotted Leroy Larron, the fence. Larron wore a three-quarter length brown leather coat, a black shirt with wide lapels and bell bottom pants that just touched the tops of his patent leather shoes that matched his hat.

They shook hands and Nate said, "Lookin' sharp, my man," thinking, *He hasn't missed a step since I went in. Here's a connection to make again.* "That hat is first class, Leroy."

Larron slid his fingers around the brim.

"Had it made by Harry the Hat Man over on William."

"Nice. You must be doing all right these days."

"Can't complain, Nate, can't complain." Looking Nate over he said, "Glad to see you're back among us, brother."

"Yeah, staying with my sister's family for now, until I get settled," Nate said, hiking up his pants.

Larron touched Nate's shoulder, edging him away from the counter and in a low voice said, "If you are so inclined, my friend, I can use a man of your talents." Looking over Nate's shoulder at the housewives at the counter, Larron said, "There are several rather loosely guarded properties that the Pythons are using for their stash in the neighborhood, you see? Places where an agile fellow might liberate items of value that I'd be interested in purchasing."

Nate nodded. Larron noticed more housewives coming into the store.

"Tell you what," Larron said. "Why don't you meet me over at the I.B.P. Club around 10:30 tonight and we'll discuss it further."

Nate nodded. *Back in business,* he thought.

15.

THE EAST SIDE, 1979

Bowie and Terrance were walking down Madison Street, eyes on the ground, but noticing everything.

"We'll pick up the package in the basement and head out through the back yard," Terrance said.

"I wish we had a fuckin' car, man," Bowie said.

"Soon, soon, man. A couple more sales and we'll will be riding in style like the Big Snake himself."

"You sure your granny doesn't know anything?"

"Not a clue. She never looks out there under the porch. Scared of spiders."

They walked up onto the wooden porch and Terrance unlocked the front door. Bowie took a last look up and down the street as they entered. *Nobody,* he thought. Once inside, Terrance suddenly stopped and slapped Bowie's chest with the back of his hand.

"Wait," he whispered. "Hear that?" They stood still and heard the sound of cracking wood coming from the back of the house. Terrance put a finger to his lips and waved them back towards the kitchen. They pulled out their switchblades. When they entered the kitchen, Nate Harwood was slowly opening the back door, pry bar in hand.

The burglar looked up and his eyes went wide when he spotted the two young men, knives in hand. He swung the pry bar at Terrance, who stepped aside and flicking open his knife, jabbed it into Nate's arm. Bowie stepped the other way and swung his blade up into the underside of Nate's jaw.

It was over in seconds, and Nate lay on the linoleum floor pumping blood. Breathing hard, Terrance said, "We gotta clean this up. Gotta get rid of the body before Granny gets home." Unconsciously, he wiped the knife blade off on his trousers.

"Shit, we gotta get rid of these clothes, too," he said, looking at the gore on himself and Bowie. "Go downstairs, Granny's got some sheets hanging up down there."

"What are we going to do about the body, man? We can't just carry it down the fuckin' street," Bowie said.

"OK, OK… Here's what we do. We take this motherfucker down in the basement. Cover it up. Clean up here. Clothes, clothes…"

"I got it!" Bowie said. "The party apartment. Over in Douglass. We got clothes there, right? We change over there, get rid of these rags. But we gotta find someone with a car to move this cocksucker," he said, kicking Nate's corpse.

"Yeah, yeah. Once we change, we'll find someone with a car, get the body before Granny gets back."

After wrapping the body in bedclothes and dropping it behind a couch in the basement, Bowie and Terrance went out the back and through the yards towards the high-rise Douglass Towers projects.

16.

THE EAST SIDE, 1979

Dunleavy pulled up half a block from the scene and watched his men operate. Detective Sergeant Maggiotto was standing in front of the house in a plaid sports coat, portable radio in hand, supervising. Neighbors would come up, trying to see inside. The patrolman on the porch kept them outside, and Maggiotto listened to what they said. *Good,* Dunleavy thought, *Listen to them all, Rico. Get the two percent that'll matter.* Detectives Kaminski and Schoetz were moving down the street, along with the district detectives canvassing the houses. Scene locked down, neighbors being canvassed. The Evidence Collection crew van was parked out front, the B.P.D. photographer's car parked directly behind. *Good, they're in there at work and my men are getting statements,* thought Dunleavy.

Dunleavy stepped out and stood by the car's door, then nodded at Maggiotto when he looked his way. The bushy haired detective sergeant scanned the scene, and assured everyone was doing their job, approached his boss.

"Chief."

"Rico. Any ID on the victim yet?"

"Not yet. Black male, late forties, early fifties. No wallet. Found in the basement. Stabbed multiple times, front and back. The

Evidence people say he's probably been dead a couple of hours. Canvass ongoing, nothing yet."

"Anything from the patrolmen on post?"

The Detective Sergeant shook his head. "Two young guys only get out of the car when they have to. They took the call, told us what they found and left after we showed up."

"This is Python territory. See any of them around?"

"Very scarce, Chief."

"You say the dead man is middle aged?"

"Yessir."

"I was reading the notices from the Parole Division. There was a burglar released from Attica last week, used to operate around here when he was out. Harwood. Nate Harwood is his name. About the right age. Check that name with the neighbors and up at the grocery store around the corner, see if anyone has seen him. The store's run by a guy named Bullock. Everybody from around here goes in there."

"Right, Chief." Maggiotto walked over to a detective just coming out of a house; they spoke for a few moments and the detective headed for the grocery store.

Dunleavy went with Maggiotto into the house and examined the crime scene as the coroner's personnel prepared to load the body onto a gurney.

"What have we got here, O'Connell?" the Chief said to the Medical Examiner.

"Middle-aged Black male, dead for less than four hours, but more than two. Cause, bled out from multiple stab wounds to the anterior and posterior abdomen, the underside of the jaw and the arm." Picking up the dead man's hands and turning them over, he said, "Defense wounds on the forearms and hands. Abrasions to the head, a couple of blood stains on the stairwell leading down here. No blood upstairs that we found yet. The back door's been jimmied, and your guys found a small crowbar in the kitchen."

"Rico," Dunleavy asked, "Who found the body?"

"Miriam Johnson. She came home, went downstairs to do some laundry and found the victim. Neighbors say she's lived here for years. They also say her grandson, Terrence Johnson, comes and goes."

"Now, there's a name we've heard before," Dunleavy said.

"Yup," Maggiotto said. "One of the Pythons' leading lights."

A Black officer in a starched uniform and lieutenant's bars on his collars came down the steps. Dunleavy turned to him and shaking his hand, said, "Ah, Calvin. Looks like we have another casualty in your precinct today."

The lieutenant looked down at the body.

"Recognize him?" Dunleavy asked.

"I believe that is our friend and neighbor Nate Harwood, Chief. I thought he was in Attica for a stretch, though."

"Just got out. Looks like he went right back to work, only he broke into the wrong house."

"Hmmph. Damn fool. Know whose house?"

"Miriam Johnson is the occupant. Her grandson Terrence has been seen in and out of here as well."

"Looks like the Python boys objected to Nate's busting into Granny Johnson's house. Surprised they left the body here, though."

"Granny came home early from bingo, found the body. I figure they wrapped Nate in this comforter and put the body behind the couch here," Dunleavy said, glancing at the other laundry hanging from clotheslines. "Figured to come back and remove the body later, but Granny comes down to check the laundry in the basement and finds Nate. She's on her way downtown now. We would like to interview Terrence and some of his associates, Calvin, if you could help scare them up. They are noticeably missing around here."

"I know all of their ratholes, Chief. I'll get all the patrolmen in the 4th on it now." He started to speak into his portable radio, then stopped and looked around.

"Where's Reynolds and Hubbert? This is on their post."

"Not present, Lt. Garrett."

"I am going to kick their goldbricking asses," Garrett said, stomping up the stairs. Garrett left the house and headed back onto the street, out of the detectives' hearing. He depressed the transmit key, waited two seconds and spoke into his portable radio quietly. *I am not going to chase those bums all over the precinct,* he thought.

"Car Four North."

"Clear."

"Have Car Four-East meet me in the side lot of the gas station at the corner of William and Jefferson, immediately if not sooner."

Garrett checked to make sure his six-point cap was on square, and thought, *I am not going to let these white boys in homicide think Lt. Garrett is some kind of token. I worked too goddamn hard for this.* When the prowl car with Reynolds and Hubbert pulled up, Garrett looked around the lot to see if anyone was watching. Satisfied they were alone, he looked at the salt and pepper team in the patrol car. "Brother" Reynolds was smiling at him from the driver's seat and Hubbert was filling out some paperwork.

"Get the fuck out of the car!" Garrett shouted. When they started to jump out, he added, "and put your hats on so at least you look like goddamn policemen you goldbricking bums!"

The two officers scrambled back into, then out of the car, putting on their hats. When they were standing in front of Garrett, the older policeman leaned towards them and pointed towards the house where the body was.

"Why the fuck aren't you on the scene over on Madison Street?"

"We stopped by, lieutenant, but—" Reynolds said.

"You, patrolmen, are going to assist in the investigation. I want to know everything that goes on with it, and not have to hear it from those headquarters dicks! Do you understand me, patrolmen?"

"Yessir," they both got out.

"You bums better get alert, and now. The homicide boys are

looking for Pythons. If you see any of that gang, take them into custody and bring them down to the station for questioning, and I don't mean maybe. Do you understand?"

They nodded.

"Now get in the fucking car and get out of my sight." As they got back in the car, Garrett added, "If I get any more surprises in my precinct like this, you'll be walking a midnight beat in the projects! Do you hear me?"

As the patrol car squealed off, Garrett got back on the radio, ordering the other cars in the precinct to rendezvous with him. *We are going to scoop those hoodlums up and shake the truth out of them before Homicide leaves the house on Madison.*

17.

Melvin Peters hung up the phone and clenched his fists in excitement. "Yes!" he said out loud, thinking of Kisha's last words to him. *"I'll meet you at the apartment in ten minutes."*

"Melvin?" Aunt Erica said.

"Uh, I'm going out for a while, Aunt Erica," Melvin said.

"When will you be back, Melvin? I'll have dinner ready around 5:30."

"Uhhh, OK," he said, checking his hair in the bathroom mirror, patting the short Afro just so, stroked his clean-shaven face and headed out for the high-rise building next to where they lived. The elevator wasn't working and he jogged up the foul-smelling project stairwell, trying to keep his feet out of the spilled liquor and broken glass. Stopping in front of the apartment door, he took a deep breath, turned the knob and entered.

"What the fuck?" Melvin said, spotting blue-jeaned Kisha standing there, raising her shoulders in puzzlement, and Terrance and Bowie pulling on clothes.

"Close the motherfuckin' door," Terrance said, zipping up his pants. "Kisha, you gotta make that shit go away," he said, nodding towards a pile of bloody clothes on the floor.

"How?" she said in a high voice.

Throwing a garbage bag at her, Terrance said, "Find a fuckin' dumpster. Somewhere outside these goddamn projects. Melvin, you didn't see anything here."

As Kisha put the clothes in the bag, Melvin said, "Whoa, man, what the hell is going on?"

Kisha shook her head and gave a fearful look at Terrance and Bowie.

"Get the hell out now, Kisha!" Terrance said.

"I'm sorry Melvin, I—" Kisha said.

"Now, bitch!" Terrance shouted, and the girl rushed out of the apartment with the trash bag. Melvin made a move to follow her.

"Stop, Melvin! Wait a minute," Bowie said. "You gotta car, Melvin?"

"Wha'? No, you know I ain't gotta car. What's going on, man? What is all this?" Melvin said.

"Look, Melvin. You gotta go down to the clubhouse. You gotta find Big Snake and tell him we need a car..." Terrance said as the door crashed open and four blue-uniformed policemen stormed in.

18.

BUFFALO POLICE HEADQUARTERS, 1979

Dunleavy got a call from the Desk Lieutenant in the 4th Precinct.

"Chief, Tom Fidele over at the 4th. Calvin Garrett's rounded up some snakes for you, all in the holding cells here. There's three of them. I think they're ready for some up close and personal conversations. I'm not sure who's more scared," he laughed, "the suspects or the patrolmen. Calvin went on a rampage after he left the scene on Madison Street."

"Great, Tom. I'll send Maggiotto to pick up one of them and have you bring the other two downtown in separate cars. I'll find out what Lt. Garrett knows when they get here."

"OK, Chief. Oh, one more thing, if anybody asks. One of the suspects fell on his way into the station."

"Tom. I need to talk to these guys, not have a lawsuit on our hands that will spring them."

"Very well, Chief. It's just sometimes they don't cooperate with the officers' commands, and…"

"Get the suspects down here in one piece, Tom."

"Will do, Chief."

When the patrolmen brought the three Pythons up to the interrogation rooms, Dunleavy looked them over. The one with the Afro and a bloody lip was cursing up a storm about police brutality and his lawyer. Looking at Maggiotto, Dunleavy said, "Rico, you talk to Mr. Johnson here in Room 1."

The next, Bowie, was a short young man, and the much taller officer accompanying him was pulling his handcuffed arms up behind him. He looked around the room, his eyes bouncing from man to man.

"Ow, ow, *owwww*, shit, man, lighten up!" he cried out.

"Room 2 for this one," Dunleavy said. "Detective Schoetz will interview him."

The third suspect wore a brown St. Bonaventure University hooded sweatshirt and kept his eyes to the ground. "Well, here's someone we haven't met yet," Dunleavy said. "Detective Kaminski has some questions for you about your afternoon's activities. Room 3."

When they were all taken into the interrogation rooms, Garrett came up to Dunleavy.

"Took us just thirty-five minutes to round these three up, Lieutenant. They were in an empty apartment in the Douglass Towers projects they use. There's a fourth one, a girl, we're still chasing, had just left the project carrying a trash bag as we got there—we figure it might hold the bloody clothes they were going to dump. I've got two patrol cars after her and the bag now."

"Excellent work, Lieutenant. Tom Fidele says one of the prisoners fell in the station house."

"Yeah, the loudmouthed one tripped coming up the steps into the station. Officers Sedziak and Downey were witnesses."

Dunleavy raised an eyebrow, but said, "Very well. Who's the quiet one? I haven't seen him before."

"That is Melvin Peters. Lives in the Douglass projects with an aunt and uncle. The others say he goes to college at Bonaventure, but here he is, hanging out with Pythons in the middle of the school year. Don't know much about him yet, haven't found any yellow sheet on him."

"Interesting. College boy to murderer," Dunleavy said.

Bowie, the suspect with the wrenched arms, massaged his wrists as Detective Schoetz took off his sport coat and hung it over the back of his chair, brushing some imaginary dust off the lapel before he sat down. He glanced at the paperwork before him, picked up a pencil and began tapping it against the table. The suspect started working the kinks out of his shoulder and stared at the detective. Schoetz kept tapping the pencil, occasionally looking at the paperwork, occasionally looking at the suspect who constantly moved around on the metal chair.

Five minutes went by, and the detective said nothing, just kept tapping the pencil and observing his prisoner.

"What?" Bowie said. The detective just shook his head. Five minutes later, Bowie said, "I want a lawyer."

"Uh huh," Schoetz said, nodding, tapping away. They could hear prisoners and police moving around out in the hallway.

"I know my rights. I want a lawyer. Now, man."

Schoetz nodded again.

More time went by, and Bowie said, "What the fuck is this, man, can't you speak? I said I want a lawyer. You have to get me one! What kind of game is this anyway?"

Schoetz smiled and kept tapping the pencil.

After a few more minutes went by, Bowie shouted, "What are we doing here, what kind of bullshit is this?"

Schoetz looked up at the clock over Bowie's head, and finally spoke. "We're waiting Mister… Bowie," checking at the paperwork in front of him. "Just waiting. When one of your partners gives you up, we'll stop waiting and you'll get locked up. It shouldn't be long now…"

"Look, that fucking old man broke into the house. He swung a crowbar at me when we cornered him, that's when I…"

Dunleavy looked in the reinforced glass window of Interrogation Room No. 1 and saw Maggiotto holding a pair of sneakers up and Terrence Johnson shouting something. Dunleavy knocked on the door, and his detective nodded and came out, holding the Adidas high top sneakers.

"What have you got, Rico?" Dunleavy said.

"Blood, Chief, blood on these sneakers."

"Is it his? That lip of his is still bleeding from his fall at the 4th."

"No, I don't think so. Look at this, Chief," he said, showing him red stains on the bottom of the sneakers. "Our man here insisted on trying to put his feet up on the table, and as I was about to knock them off, I spotted the blood stains on the bottom here. My guess is they may have come from the victim."

"Lt. Garrett is chasing a girl down now who might've taken all their bloody clothes away from the apartment. Are you saying they missed these?"

"Expensive sneakers, Adidas Top Tens. My guess is they didn't spot the blood, and this dummy didn't throw them away."

"Very good, Rico. We'll take these as evidence and see what Central Police Services comes up with."

Dunleavy walked over to Room Three, where the third suspect sat in the brown collegiate hoodie and faded bell bottoms, shaking his head. Dunleavy knocked on the door and Kaminski came out.

"Whaddaya got, Ski?"

"Not much. This one," Kaminski said, jerking his thumb towards the soundproof door, where Melvin Peters was handcuffed to the table. "This Melvin Peters guy denies having been at the scene of the murder at all. Says he was just at the empty apartment to meet a girl and these other guys were already there. Wants to tell his aunt and uncle where he is so they can come get him. I don't think he realizes how much trouble he's in."

Dunleavy looked at the suspect inside, who was craning his neck to see out the tiny reinforced window in the door. *Peters. Melvin*

Peters, he thought, *that name's familiar for some reason.*

"All right, keep at him. He's supposed to be a student at Bonny? Ask him why he's not there, then come back to the Harwood killing. You know the routine to get him off guard."

Kaminski nodded, went back to the interrogation room and removed the suspect's handcuffs. He sat down on the corner of the table as Melvin slid back into the chair, jamming his hands in the hoodie pocket.

"Well Melvin, I think it's too bad about you not being at Bonaventure—you were at East High before that, right?"

"No. I was at Bennett."

"You musta got good grades there to get into Bona."

"Yeah."

"Well, they're not going to help you now. And I don't think we'll need to call your aunt and uncle, because you're going to jail for the murder of Nate Harwood."

"I didn't kill anyone, man. There was no body in that apartment. Nobody got killed there. I told you, I was just there to meet a girl, man."

"Well, maybe she can help you out, Melvin, and verify your story," the detective said, looking off at a notice on the wall. "If you tell me her name, we can check it out."

Melvin shook his head. "Uh, uh. I… I'm not sure what her name is."

"C'mon, Melvin, you were going to meet this girl in private, and you don't know her name?"

"I'm not sure, she just went by her initial, K, you know?"

"Well, how about where she lives? Just the block will do…"

"She lives over by North Division Street somewheres…"

19.

BUFFALO POLICE HEADQUARTERS, 1979

Dunleavy looked at what he had and took it to the Assistant D.A. "I've got one guy blabbing when he got pissed off, a grandmother who's not saying anything about her grandson, but he's been in and out of the house where the killing happened. Two of the suspects were changing their clothes when Garrett caught them in the projects, a third guy who says he was only at the apartment to meet a girl, and a girl we can't find or identify who probably dumped the bloody clothes and a pair of switchblades we found in a dumpster near the apartment. We also sent the one guy's sneakers off to the lab to check the blood on them. I'll bet you dollars to donuts the blood will match Nate Harwood and not Terrance Johnson."

"Well, Chief," the lawyer said, "if the blood does match the victim's, and if he doesn't happen to have the same blood type as Johnson, I think we have a case against him and Bowie. You got lucky when you tracked the girl's probable path from the projects home and found the clothes and the knives. Keep trying to track the girl down, but the bloody clothes' sizes match that of Bowie and Johnson, and we're checking for hair and other evidence. The knives were wiped but we may find something there yet. All we can nail Peters for is as an accessory to the fact, criminal trespass and concealing evidence of a crime."

Dunleavy knocked on the door to the interrogation room, and Kaminski came out.

"Whaddaya got, Ski?"

"He keeps saying nobody got killed in that apartment and he was there to meet some girl. He's not giving anybody up, just the vicinity where he thinks she lives, like he said."

"Here's what we've got so far—blood on the clothes, blood on the shoes and the one guy's shooting his mouth off. So far, nothing ties this kid into the murder. Let me talk to him a little, play the good guy. You knock on the door in a few minutes and we'll do the nod and whisper routine."

"Right, Chief," Ski said, and opened the door for the senior policeman. Melvin looked up and put his hands on the table. Dunleavy opened the folder Kaminski had given him and began to read to himself, a delaying tactic that Schoetz and the rest of the Homicide Squad had learned from him.

Melvin Peters, age 18, lives in the Projects with his aunt and uncle. Father unaccounted for, mother killed in a liquor store robbery in 1970 shootout between hold up men and store owner. Now I remember, *Dunleavy thought.* The owner had a shotgun, the robbers pistols. Lead must have been flying everywhere, blood was all over the place. I caught that case. Had to notify the aunt and uncle as next of kin and they got custody of the little boy. He didn't cry out loud, just tears all down his face. This is him now, huh?

"Melvin Peters, age eighteen. No prior encounters with the law, is that correct?"

"Yes," Melvin answered.

"You know we're going to check on that, right?"

"Yeah, I know. It's true. I've never been arrested."

"You live with your aunt and uncle there in the projects, right?"

"Yes," he said, his eyes dancing, "I told that other cop that already."

"Graduated Bennett High School and attended Bonaventure for

a while… you got kicked out for having drugs in the dorm, right? See, we have friends all over. One phone call down there and we found that out. Not a good career move, Melvin."

Melvin remained silent.

"I don't think you were in on the killing on Madison Street, but you're going to have to do better to not go down with Johnson and Bowie, Melvin. We've got them dead to rights. They might get life in Attica for this and take you down with them. Attica's not a nice place for a young guy like you."

Kaminski knocked on the door, and when Dunleavy opened it, the detective nodded at Melvin, then whispered to his Chief. Dunleavy turned and looked at Melvin, then reclosed the door.

"Last chance, Melvin. Detective Kaminski has just told me of some new evidence we've found, and it doesn't look good for you…"

After another half an hour of questioning, Melvin hadn't changed his story; the D.A.'s assistant told Dunleavy they'd charge Melvin with what they had, but he was doubtful they could make the accessory to murder charge stick.

"Look at this, Steve, the damn kid's shaking," the identification tech said to the clerk as he gripped Melvin's hand above the cardboard fingerprint form. "Shouldn't do the crime if you can't do the time, kid," he added as Melvin thought about the bad shit he'd heard happens "inside" from guys in the neighborhood who'd been there.

20.

KOREA, 1950

Andy and Corporal Manet shoved their heads as far into the frozen mud they could push them when the blast showered them with dirt and rocks. *Closer this time,* Andy thought. He heard Manet muttering a prayer. It sounded like that psalm about the valley of death. *We're on a mountain, you fool,* he thought as another explosion rocked the foxhole and Manet curled up in a fetal position. Andy waited. *The shelling usually lasts four or five minutes,* he thought, *and it's been about two or so.* When the shelling ended, they heard the bugles start blowing and Manet said, "The Commie bastards are coming now." Manet cautiously stuck his head up over the edge of the foxhole and shouted to the machine gun emplacement to their right.

"Harrington! Killen! You all right?"

No reply.

"Are you guys ready? The sons of bitches are coming up the hill!" he screamed as the bugles grew louder. He ducked back down in the hole.

"Something's wrong. Maybe a shell got them. Harrington! Killen! What the hell are you doing?" he yelled. Now they could year the Chinese infantry's high-pitched screams coming from just down the slope.

"You gotta cover me," Andy said, shaking Manet's shoulder as he grabbed his M-1 rifle and leapt out of the hole.

"I gotcha, Andy, I gotcha," Manet said. He stood up and started spraying the descending slope with bullets from his Thompson gun. *Good boy,* Andy thought.

In the other foxhole, Andy found Harrington, eyes wide open and his mouth agape. Killen was on his face, his bloodied field jacket shredded by shrapnel. The .30 caliber machine gun was knocked askew and its ammunition belt tangled.

"Keep 'em off me!" he shouted to Manet as he worked to untangle the belt. Manet slammed another magazine into the Thompson and fired in an arc in front of the foxhole knocking down two Chinese soldiers about to throw grenades. When the burst ended, two other soldiers in quilted coats came forward with burp guns, one blasting Manet back into the foxhole, the other rushing towards Andy's foxhole. Andy shot him and ducked low, then spotting the other burp gunner approaching the edge of his foxhole, rammed his bayonet into the soldier's groin and shoved him off to the left. He spun forward just as a teenage infantryman pulled the trigger on his rifle and discovered they hadn't given him any bullets. His eyes went wide, he screamed and lunged forward with his bayonet. Andy parried the weapon with his M-1 and heard the cartilage in the boy's neck crackle as his own bayonet ended the kid's life. A quick look down the hill told him he had a few seconds. He repositioned the .30 caliber, laid the ammunition belt out straight just as an illumination round burst overhead, revealing a horde of soldiers struggling up the hill in an eerie white glow. Depressing the .30 caliber's barrel, he fired off a few well aimed bursts, dropping the nearest Chinese attackers. Then mortar rounds started falling into the approaching Chinese infantry, and a few moments later Andy heard the whoosh of 105 mm artillery coming overhead, and the explosions drowned out the screams. The bugles of the attackers went silent. Andy looked carefully down the hill and held his fire as the Chinese retreated from his kill zone into the darkness. Glancing at the dead teenager, he noticed the boy had no socks, his ulcerated feet shod in ragged canvas tennis shoes. He knocked the boy's feet off the edge of his foxhole and peered down into the darkness, hearing the groans of the wounded. Another flare went up and Andy fired down into the ones that moved. Assured that none were a threat, he looked over at the foxhole to his right and shouted, "Manet!" No response. *Must be dead,* he thought. He fed another belt into the machine gun and settled down to wait for reinforcements to arrive.

21.

BUFFALO CENTRAL TERMINAL, THE EAST SIDE, 1951

Andy got off the train at Central Station and lugged his barracks bag down the platform and up into the main concourse. The station was crowded with people swiftly crossing the marble floors in all directions under the buff tiled arches as the station announcer called out the arrivals and departures in a clipped voice. Olive drab uniforms like his were everywhere, and he stood there for a moment, looking for anyone he might recognize, then picked up his bag, headed out of the terminal and got in a Checker cab. The driver turned, examining his uniform.

"You kill plenty of Communists, soldier?" the driver said in a Polish accent.

"A bunch," Andy answered.

"Where to?" the driver said. "It's on the house."

Andy hesitated for a second, thinking of his wheezing father and the rickety cottage on Moreland Street, and said, "Hotel Huron," knowing of a comfortable bed and the proximity of whores in the neighborhood.

22.

LOVEJOY, THE EAST SIDE, 1952

Andy turned off the grinder at five, dropping the sharpened restaurant knives into the wooden box. As he was pulling on his coat, Gambacorta, the owner, shouted, "Hey wait a second." He gathered up several other knives, wrapped them in a cloth, and handed them to Andy.

"Stop by the bar on Ideal on your way home and drop these off, will ya? And here," Gambacorta said, pulling a dollar and two quarters out, "have some supper and a couple beers on me while you're there. Thanks, Andy."

Andy touched the bill to his head, tucked the package under his arm and headed out into the darkening evening. He headed straight for the bar with thoughts of hot food, while his dad poked at the fire in the Franklin stove and scratched the puppy's head hoping Andy would be home soon to fix his supper.

Inside, the bar was full and the atmosphere warm with steam heat. Andy sat down at a tiny table, taking off his coat and laying the wrapped knives down. He waved to Franco, the owner, who nodded and kept pouring shots and beers for the after-work crowd of railroad shop men like his father. *This is where he wants me to stay,* he thought. *Working in the neighborhood, living in that shack and taking care of him forever.*

At the table next to him, a bull-necked man and a jittery guy had small glasses of something clear that smelled like licorice in front of them, speaking in low voices. The bull-necked man nodded at the front door as a man in a brown suit entered. The jittery guy turned around to look. The man in the brown suit noticed and stiffened, smoothed his hair back. Bull neck motioned him over with three fingers. He came over slowly, his head bowed and stood in front of T's table.

"You have something for me, yes?" T said, Twitch turning towards the brown suit. The brown suit said nothing.

"I have come all the way from Niagara Falls to see you, Gregory. I hope you are not wasting my time."

Gregory looked around and remained silent, and Twitch stood up. Gregory stepped back, bumping into a bar customer.

"Let's go outside where it's not so crowded," T said, pointing towards the rear of the bar. The three of them started walking back, Gregory leading, glancing over his shoulder.

"Whaddaya got for me, kid?" Franco said to Andy from the bar. Andy looked away from the three men leaving and carried his package to the owner, laying it on the bar. Franco unwrapped it, nodded, and took some change from the register. Andy was giving him a receipt when Gregory slugged Twitch and ran past T, followed by two big men who had just come in the back door.

"What the hell?" Franco said as Gregory was pulling a revolver from his coat and crashed into Andy. Andy grabbed Gregory's gun hand with his left, snatched up a carving knife off the bar with his right and ran it under Gregory's sternum. Gregory gasped, people who turned to see what was happening started yelling, and the two big men grabbed Gregory and dragged him quickly out the back, knife in his chest and his legs collapsing underneath him. T stared at Andy, then followed the others out the back.

"What the hell was that all about?" one patron said from his barstool.

"Looked like that bookie, that Gregory guy, started an argument, but that guy at the bar slugged him and those other guys dragged him outside," said another.

"Holy shit. That's crazy! What's that all about?" said a third.

"None of my business," said another customer at the bar, and the men who bet with Gregory returned to their drinks.

"Stay put," Franco told Andy, coming out from behind the bar and heading out back. A few moments later, Franco came back in and said to the patrons, "Don't worry. Everything's all right. Just a little squabble," then, whispering to Andy, "Mr. T wants to talk to you outside."

Andy furrowed his brow and looked at Franco.

"It's OK, Andy, everything's fine. The man wants to thank you," he said, slapping him on the back.

Andy went outside, where one car was pulling away and Twitch was sitting behind the wheel of the purple Cadillac. T stood next to the car, and when Twitch nodded, T turned to Andy and smiled.

"Very good, very good," T said as he approached Andy, his hand outstretched. Andy took it slowly. Wagging his free index finger at Andy, T continued, "That crazy man could've hurt somebody, maybe even killed somebody, young man. My friends," he said, nodding towards the sedan as it pulled away, "are taking him to a doctor. Did you know this Gregory, young man?"

Andy shook his head. Clapping his hands on both Andy's shoulders, he nodded and said, "You move very quickly and stopped that foolishness, my friend. You have some fighting experience?"

"In Korea."

"Ah, I see, in that war. Very good. You have nerve, young man. Franco tells me you work for Mario, the grinding shop. How much do you make there, young man…"

23.

LOVEJOY, 1952

Andy's first job for Mr. T was with Twitch. Twitch met him in front of Stypa's coal yard on Krupp Street around 3:00 a.m., driving a rusted-out Plymouth.

"Put your gloves on," he told Andy.

"Where did you get this jalopy?" Andy asked him as the engine coughed.

"Don't worry, it'll get the job done," Twitch, said, his neck muscles contracting, pulling his shoulder to his neck. Watching Twitch contort, Andy thought, *Do the job, get the money.*

"This guy kept taking loans out on his business. He signed over the license to us for the last one and he won't pay back the rest." Twitch didn't say another word as they drove south out of the city on Route 16, winding through the silent country villages until they passed a well-lit tavern. They slowed about fifty feet past the bar and pulled over behind a barn. Twitch shut the engine down and they sat, Twitch looking around.

"Now what?" Andy asked.

"We wait a few minutes, see if anyone's around. This guy stays open until four, even if there's no one in the bar. He keeps his car out back. That's where we get him."

They waited, and Twitch kept checking his watch.

"Isn't this Jack Cole's, the football player's joint?" Andy asked.

"Yes," Twitch said. "He thinks he's a tough guy, that we can't collect the rest of the money from him." He looked over at Andy, watching for a reaction. Andy sat there, his hands in his jacket pockets. Then, looking at his watch, Twitch said, "It's time."

They got out of the car, quietly closed the doors and approached the back door of the bar. Twitch handed Andy a .22 caliber revolver.

"Only use that if we have to. Noise travels far out here in the country. You get behind his car, then show yourself when I signal."

Jack Cole, a big man with blonde thinning hair, came out of the bar's back door whistling, and pulling out a big set of keys, triple locked it. *He's whistling that Frank Sinatra song, "Young at Heart,"* Andy thought. When Cole turned and approached the car, Twitch nodded to Andy from the shadows, and Andy stood up, the pistol out of sight behind his leg. The big man jerked to a halt.

"Who the hell're you?" Cole growled. Twitch stepped forward and hit him with a piece of pipe, but the blow glanced off his head and landed mostly on his shoulder. As Twitch tried to swing the pipe again, the bigger man spun and backhanded Twitch, knocking him against the building. Andy rushed forward, and remembering Twitch's warning, bashed Cole on the head with the pistol. Cole hunched his shoulders up as the hairless skin on the back of his head opened and blood ran, but the big man growled and turned, his face contorted in pain and anger, his hands reaching for Andy like bear claws. Andy stepped back and swung his right foot as hard as he could into Cole's groin. Cole winced and dropped to his knees. Twitch got up and slammed the pipe on the downed man's head once, and then a second time as the football player pitched forward. Out of breath Twitch said, "Quick, go get the car."

When Andy came up with the car, he saw Twitch grunting, pulling on a section of piano wire wrapped around Cole's thick neck.

"He's already dead, you goof," Andy said.

"Get… the… blankets… out of the trunk," Twitch gasped.

They wrapped the football player up in the blankets, and Andy saw lengths of heavy chain in the trunk when they loaded him in there. They drove both cars back towards Buffalo, first leaving Cole's car unlocked with the keys in it along an empty section of Southwestern Boulevard outside the village of Hamburg. Then driving the Plymouth into Buffalo, they went along Tifft Road past a welding shop and down an undeveloped street with a marsh on one side, where they stopped. They wrapped the blanket-covered body in chains and submerged the dead bar owner in a pond.

When they were a mile away from the pond, Twitch exhaled and his spasms subsided.

"You did a good job. The man will be pleased," he said.

"I did better than that," Andy said. "I saved your ass back there." Twitch's jaw clenched, then Andy said, "When and where do I get paid?"

"I'll meet you by the coal yard, where I picked you up, tomorrow night. You'll get your money then."

"What about the car?" Andy asked.

"It's gotta get lost," he said, pulling up a block away from Andy and his father's cottage. He reached past Andy and opened the car door.

"Tomorrow at seven at the coal yard," he said, shut the door and drove off. Andy felt the heft of the pistol in his pocket. *The spastic forgot to take this back. I'll stash it under the floorboards in the house,* he thought.

24.

THE WEST SIDE, BUFFALO, 1955

Two guys, one in a tailored charcoal suit with silvering hair and hooded eyes and a guy about Andy's age in a flannel shirt and cardigan sweater, were sitting alone at the end of the bar. The suit drank that licorice drink and the younger guy whiskey. The older guy looked Andy over as he approached and the younger guy threw down his drink.

"You're the soldier who lives in Lovejoy?" the older man said in a voice just above a whisper.

"Yeah, I'm Andy Rakestraw," he said, putting his hand out.

"Grant Strozzare," he said, shaking it. "This is Zeno LaPancia."

The younger guy jumped off the stool, nodded and shook his hand.

"I'm Z," he said. Andy noticed he was sweating and breathing rapidly. The suit flicked a piece of dust off the crease in his pants and got up.

"Let's go," he said and led them out into the parking lot, where they got into a big Chrysler Imperial. Z drove, and Strazzo lit up a Chesterfield.

Turning his head slightly to the left, Strazzo said, "We're headed to the Union Hall. A man there is causing problems. He changes the records at night in the basement to hide what he steals…"

"He's runs the insurance plan…" Z said.

Strazzo looked at Z and he shut up.

"You and Z will clobber him, then I'll tell you what to do."

In the parking lot out back, Strazzo gave Z the keys to the hall. They entered and walked down the steps to the basement and along a hall way where one office was lit. Z handed Andy a pair of gloves and donned a pair himself. The three of them stopped in front of the office, and a bald man with a pencil mustache looked up from a file cabinet.

"Hey, what are you guys doing…" Z rushed him and punched him in the face, then grabbed him around the neck and slammed his head into the cabinet. As he held him there, Strazzo said to Andy, "Get his keys."

The bald man struggled as Z kept the grip around his neck and Andy checked his pockets. That done, Strazzo said, "Gag him," and handed Andy a long cloth which he tied around the man's mouth as he struggled.

"Now, upstairs."

Andy and Z dragged the man while Strazzo followed. When they had him on the mat in the rear hallway, Z and Andy pummeled him until he groaned and stopped struggling. Strazzo dropped a length of rope in front of them.

"Now, tie him up like I tell you—Z, make the noose around his neck the way I showed you… you, Lovejoy, bend his legs back towards his head, yes. Z, bring the rope back and tie it around his ankles… tighter. Tighter! Now, Lovejoy, go get his car—the red Chevy in the parking lot."

Strazzo watched, smoking another Chesterfield, as they manhandled the whimpering man into the trunk of the Chevy.

"The more he struggles, the tighter it gets," Z said to Andy. Z drove the Chrysler and Andy followed in the Chevy. They pulled into The Curtiss-Wright Aircraft plant lot and looked around. The airplane factory was silent.

"Nothing going on here since the war," Z said as Andy got into the back of the Chrysler, leaving the Chevy. When they drove back to the bar, Strazzo set up two whiskeys and an anisette.

"Salute," Strazzo said, and they drank the shots down. Turning to Andy, Strazzo pulled an envelope from his coat pocket, and handing it to him said, "Good work." Andy took the money and left. Z blinked but asked no questions.

The next night, Strazzo and the rest of his crew were standing in the back room of a restaurant on Hampshire Street and each one embraced Z, who arrived smiling in a double-breasted navy suit with a silk handkerchief in the breast pocket. His hair oiled, he bowed slightly when T stood up and embraced him.

The room silent, Strazzo handed T a long shining dagger with four sides. T took Z's right hand and jabbed Z's index finger, saying, "You must never betray any of the secrets of the family. You must never violate the wife or child of a member of the family. You must never use narcotics."

Z looked T in the eye, but noticed his blood was dripping onto a plate with a holy card like the ones given to him as a child. It was a picture of St. Francis of Assisi. Next to it was an old Webley .45 revolver. Strazzo set the holy card on fire.

Z repeated what he had memorized in Italian. "As a member of the family, I will die and burn like this Saint before I betray a member of this family. I will use any means, like this gun and this knife, to be strong for the family. I am a member of this family forever."

The weapons, plate and ashes of the holy card were removed and everyone again embraced Z. They filed out to the dining room where a long table was prepared. While they were eating, Z was told the legend of the Webley pistol and the dagger.

"The first one killed was the pharmacist, on Busti. He refused to help our family when one was injured. T and our former *consigliore* had that knife and that gun. They killed him in his house, and the Don brings it for the ceremony, to remind everyone of the seriousness of our business, and how long we have been together."

Later, after the wine was flowing, Z asked if Lovejoy would be admitted. Strazzo overheard the question from a distance. Everyone grew silent.

"Never. He is *straniero*. An outsider. T has made him a friend of his, but not a friend of the family. We must keep the old traditions and only let *Italo* in the family."

T nodded, and pointing with his index finger around the room, said, "To be strong, we must stay close."

So, they get this guy Andy to do a job and just pay him like he fixed your car? Z thought.

Z refilled his glass and just listened for the rest of the dinner.

Z saw Andy a week later at the bar.

"Hey, Andy!" Z said, waving him over. "Have a drink. This…" he said to the white-aproned bartender, "is my friend Andy," putting his hand on Andy's shoulder.

"Danny Lerzak," the bartender said, shaking his hand.

"Andy," he said in a low tone.

"Two shots of your best Canadian, Danny boy."

They toasted each other. Andy noticed people were walking up to Z to say hello and nodding to him as they left the bar.

"You're popular these days," Andy said.

"Yeah, ain't I?" Z said. He leaned in close and added, "it's all because of the job we did that night."

"They know about that?"

"Naw. But they know I'm in the family now. I got made because of it. That's why they're all looking, saying hello."

"Hmm. Now me, I don't want them to look at all," Andy

whispered. "Cheers," Andy said, and putting down his shot glass, added, "Thanks for the cocktail, Z. Good luck, I gotta run."

"All right, my man. You gotta stop by when you get some time. Hey, Danny, see if you can fix the horizontal hold on the TV, the Yankees are coming on the Game of the Week."

25.

THE WEST SIDE, 1956

After the job with Strazzo and Z, Andy got his first solo job. It was a truck driver who smuggled things for the mob, sometimes morphine stolen from a pharmacy in Hamilton across the Canadian border. When he started selling off some of the goods and keeping some of the morphine to support his own habit, Twitch noticed his pinpoint eyes and his constant scratching. Squalo noticed his reduced deliveries.

Taking coffee in the back room of the café on Jersey Street, T said to Squalo, Strazzo and Twitch, "We must make the driver go away, then replace him with somebody reliable."

"Right, Mr. T," Twitch said.

"Use that man, the one from Lovejoy for this," T said.

Twitch nodded and left.

When he was gone, T took a sip of coffee and said to his younger underlings, "This will work well. This Lovejoy takes care of the problem, he's not one of us, nobody knows him. He gets his pay, like Twitch, but he's not *cosa nostra*, isn't family like you boys."

They nodded.

"But that means he's not loyal like us, Mr. T," Squalo said after a pause.

"I know this kind of man," T said. "He is very cold. All he wants is money. But he also knows our power is everywhere. He knows he must stay quiet about our arrangement."

Twitch drove his 1956 Buick to meet Andy in the parking lot of Immaculate Conception School on Elmwood. Andy arrived in a used Chevy Styleline.

"So, you bought a car," Twitch said.

Andy smiled, "I've been saving up."

Twitch gave him the details: who the driver was, the company he worked for, his route, his habits.

"So, when?" Twitch asked.

Lovejoy shook his head. "This has got to be done carefully. I'll have to follow him, watch him, set this up." Looking Twitch right in the eyes, he said, "I'm not like you guys, I gotta work for a living. The trucking company is one of T's businesses, right? When this driver doesn't show up for work, you'll know it's done." He brushed a leaf off the hood of his car, got in the Chevy and drove away.

26.

THE WEST SIDE, 1956

Twitch started following Lovejoy around after his last smart-ass remark. *I don't trust this son of a bitch,* he thought, as he followed the Chevy from the grinder's shop to the truck stop on Ohio Street. The driver stopped in there regularly on his way back from a run. He noticed Lovejoy always parked his car where he could watch all the drivers come and go.

Thursdays, Lovejoy thought, *that's the day when he makes the run up to Hamilton and gets the dope.* Lovejoy followed him from the diner back to the garage to park the truck. Then the driver took his own car over to Broderick Park on the Niagara River. The driver sat in his car for a while, then got out of it and sat on the benches for a long time just looking at the swift Niagara River roll on towards the Falls. *He must get high in his car, then come watch the water,* he thought. The driver stayed there for a long time, and Lovejoy watched as the local fishermen reeled in their lines, picked up their buckets and left at sundown. *Just right,* he thought.

The following Thursday, the driver followed his routine, but when he got to the park, there were bread crumbs spread all along the benches at the south end of the park and pigeons swarming all around them. He walked north towards the water treatment plant and was almost there when he finally found a bench where there weren't any birds. He sat down, his mind drifting into the euphoric morphine high as he watched the river flow and the sun slowly settle down in the red sky across the river in Canada.

Lovejoy watched from a distance, and seeing the driver dozing, drove slowly up behind the benches. Quietly getting out of the car, he approached the bench from behind, and after giving a last look around, swung the lead filled sap against the back of the driver's head. As the driver slumped over, Lovejoy dragged him over to the iron railing at the river's edge where he'd left a piece of steel I-beam earlier. He tied the I-beam with a stout cord around his victim's neck. Draping the body over the railing, he swiftly heaved the I-beam into the river and flipped the limp body after it.

Done. Not a trace left. They'll never find him in a million years down there, Lovejoy thought as he watched the water tumble by as if nothing had happened. He looked around, then suddenly stopped as he heard the sound of cracking wood. He looked up, and there was a kid about seven years old in a stunted tree behind him. Dressed in a green and white striped T-shirt and oversized blue jeans, the kid pulled his legs up when he saw Lovejoy looking at him.

"Hey son, whaddaya doing up there?" Lovejoy said with a smile, slowly approaching the tree. *He's as high up as he can go in that little tree,* he thought.

"Did you see me help that guy into the river? He's gonna come up in just a minute with a musket the British dropped down there during the War of 1812. Wanna help me when he comes back up?"

The kid shook his head and tried to climb higher. Now at the base of the tree, Lovejoy grabbed the boy's leg and yanked him down. The boy started to scream, but Lovejoy covered his mouth. Looking around and seeing no one, Lovejoy carried the child over to the river, banged his head hard against the iron railing and heaved him into the river, where the boy went into the swift water and disappeared.

I don't believe it, Twitch thought, watching from his parked car on Niagara Street. *He just killed that little boy like he was nothing.*

27.

THE WEST SIDE, 1956

On Saturday morning over coffee at the café, T chuckled when Squalo told him the driver didn't show up for work on Friday, and no one could get hold of him. He looked over at Twitch, who was reading the paper at a table by the front window. "Pack a nice lunch for our friend Lovejoy." Then he told Squalo, "And you, this time, hire somebody *reliable* for the Canadian route." Squalo put down his coffee, said, "OK, boss," and left.

"Strazzo," T said, "You keep an eye on the deliveries from Canada from now on. This means good money for us and there will be more later if we handle this right."

Twitch folded up his newspaper and hesitated, thinking about telling T what he'd just read. T looked at him, and he hesitated no more, leaving to find Lovejoy.

Twitch met Lovejoy in the parking lot of the big clapboarded tavern on Bailey under a sign that read House Of Beef. As he handed him the paper grocery bag with the money, he said, "Did you see today's paper?"

"Sure," Lovejoy said. "The Yankees won. Made me twenty bucks."

"No, I meant on the front page. About the kid."

"Not yet, I always go to the sports section first."

"The kid whose body washed up in the piers at Jafco Marina."

"No I didn't see that. Here, lemme look," he said, clutching the satchel of money down between his legs and taking the folded newspaper from under Twitch's arm.

"Hmm, 'Missing Plymouth Avenue Boy Found in River—Gary Atkings of Plymouth Avenue was found this morning by boaters at the foot of Hertel Avenue. The cause of death is believed to be drowning, although the autopsy report is not final. His parents, Roberta and Harvey Atkings…' Gee, that's tragic Twitch. Did you know the family?"

"You know what I mean. I saw you…"

"Ah, what, are you going crazy or something? Hey look, I'm going in here for some shrimp cocktail to celebrate. C'mon, I'll buy you a beef and a cocktail," he said, smiling, trying to turn the jittery man towards the restaurant. Twitch pulled himself loose.

"Get away from me, you're sick, you bastard."

Lovejoy stood there, arms extended, palms up. "What? I did the job, everything's covered, forget it. C'mon, have a drink, Twitch." Twitch turned and walked away. Lovejoy shrugged, put the satchel in the trunk of his car and went into the restaurant. Over his shrimp cocktail, he thought about the money in the bag. It was enough to quit his job and move out of the cottage. Yeah. The Hotel Huron. That's where he'd go. Nightlife downtown and hookers.

28.

UNIVERSITY HEIGHTS, NORTH BUFFALO, 1979

Adele was putting the eggs on the plates with her new Teflon spatula when Leo came in the kitchen, rubbing his hands together.

"Ah, just what the doctor ordered," he said, "scrambled eggs and..." sniffing the air, "bacon."

Jimmy was reaching for the plate where the bacon was wrapped in paper towels when Adele said, "Jimmy, wait 'til your father sits down before you start snatching the bacon."

"Bridget, would you say grace, please," Leo said as both parents sat down. Bridget folded her hands, closed her eyes and said the prayer as Jimmy sat with hands poised over the plate with the bacon. Adele shook her head. Leo sighed and tucked a napkin in under his chin, covering a blue silk necktie.

"You're wearing the tie I got you for your birthday," Cecile said.

"And a very nice one it is," Leo said, waiting until the children had snatched up the bacon they wanted.

"I guess you'll be in court today for the sentencing, right dad?" Cecile said.

"Uh, yes, that's right, Ceelee," Leo said.

"I read it in the news last night," she said.

"Why so curious about dad's work these days, Ceelee?" Adele said.

"Well, it's a big case, and Dad put it together. If it hadn't been for Dad…"

"Now, that's not true, Cecile," Leo said. "There were any number of people that put that case together—Mr. Maggiotto and the rest of his shift in Homicide, the scene investigation unit, the crime scene photography unit, the patrolmen in the 4th Precinct, the coroner, the lawyers in the prosecutor's office…"

"Yeah, but you were the one who knew who the dead man was and who the most likely suspects were…"

"How did you know that, daughter of mine?" Leo said, looking at Adele.

"I heard you talking on the phone with the assistant district attorney. Hey, Jimmy, leave that last piece of bacon for Bridget!"

29.

ELMIRA CORRECTIONAL FACILITY, 1979

Melvin Peters knew it was a bad place, but he didn't realize how bad a place a maximum-security prison was until he started getting processed into Elmira. The bus drove past a bronze statue of two men covered only with fig leaves, where employees walked on wide steps in and out of a brick building with a green copper roof at the top of a grassy hill. The bus continued around to the back of the prison and stopped in a lot surrounded by high fences topped with razor wire. The convicts were led across a gray concrete lot under the watchful eyes of a guard with an AR-15 rifle behind tinted glass in a tower, then through a square tunnel made of more chain link fencing covered by triple razor wire and passed into the Reception Center where Marvin was led through the stations.

After showering and delousing, Melvin was given a shave and a haircut, issued his green inmate clothes, photographed and assigned a Department Identification Number. Then he stood behind a four-foot block wall and was told to remove his clothes. "Bend over and spread 'em," the big country boy officer told him. Thinking of the bronze statue outside, Melvin hesitated.

"It is not an option, inmate. The body cavity search will be conducted one way or another."

Pulling down his trousers, Melvin said, "Easy, easy there, officer.

I'm cooperating."

As he was led into the three-tier corridor, the occupants stared at him with narrowed eyes. Melvin noticed one cell where a man was laying on his bunk, face burrowed into a red stained pillow. They stopped at the next one-man cell.

"Stop," the guard ordered, who then said, "Open 315," into his portable radio. When the blue-barred door opened, Melvin entered and placed his folded bedding and other possessions on the bunk in the white cell. A metal sink and toilet were bolted to the concrete wall, and a single fluorescent light hummed overhead.

When the barred door closed, the guard stepped back to where the bloodied inmate lay on the bunk.

"You all right?" the guard asked.

"Yes," was mumbled through the pillow, and the guard went back to the Intake Center.

Melvin arranged his possessions and listened to the talk on the tier. When he finished with the blanket he sat on the bunk and whispered to his bloodied neighbor.

"Hey, you all right, man?"

"Will be."

"Guards get rough?"

"Naw."

"Don't worry about him, new man," a deep bass voice growled from down the corridor, cutting through the coughs and grunts and shrieks, "unless you want a real initiation party."

30.

ELMIRA CORRECTIONAL FACILITY, 1979

The next day, Melvin found the source of the bass voice in the shower room. He went in with five other guys, and as he went around the edge of the tiled and humid room, he heard that bass voice again.

"Now," the voice said, and four guys grabbed Melvin's limbs and pinned him face first against the tiled wall under a shower head.

"OK, Mister Python," the voice said. "Welcome to Elmira. Down here, the Harlem Cats are in charge, and there's a lot more of us here than your penny-ante projects gang could even count. Now, we can work this a couple of ways. You can cooperate and join our congregation, or you can try to join up with some bunch of fleas here. If you do try to join up with them, we might not appreciate your presence," and with that, one of the men holding him pulled his head back by the hair and they all shoved his face up into the hot water flowing from the shower head.

"No, no, I can cooperate, I can cooperate. I'm just trying to get along, just get through this," Melvin said.

"A correct decision, Python. But don't forget and change your mind," the voice said, and with that, Melvin felt a toothbrush begin to penetrate his anus. "Because we're always around."

"No, no, I won't forget, I won't forget," and he felt the toothbrush withdraw.

"Good. Brethren, welcome Mr. Python here to Elmira," and with that, the four men let him go and started throwing punches to his body and the back of his head. When they finished, Melvin looked up from the shower floor and saw the four of them troop out, his head buzzing and his eyes struggling to focus. The source of the voice stood at the entrance. He was light skinned, built like a lightweight boxer and one eye was sightless and cloudy. He was only about five six, and that was including his two-inch Afro.

"I'm the leader of this congregation, Python. They call me Adze. Don't forget it," and he disappeared as a guard started shouting, "C'mon, c'mon get your asses outta there and get dressed…"

As he staggered to his feet, Melvin thought, *One to three years was the sentence. The lawyer said if I kept out of trouble, they'd let me out after two on conditional release. How the hell do you stay out of trouble in this place?*

31.

ELMIRA CORRECTIONAL FACILITY, 1979

Melvin spoke to the man from the adjoining cell out on the exercise yard. He too had been recently initiated by the Harlem Cats, and always seemed to be trying to hide—from the gangs, the guards, from himself, Melvin figured. His name was Anton, and he was from the Bronx. He had gotten caught riding with his cousin in a stolen car, and when they got pulled over, the cops found a gun between the seats and Anton got one to three years, like Melvin.

"How about you?" Anton asked as they ambled around the yard avoiding the stares of the weightlifters, the bikers and the other several gangs if they got close. "I heard them call you 'college boy.' Is that real?"

"Started to," Melvin said. "I was at Bonaventure. Some friends of mine from home came down to Olean one weekend and brought some weed with them. We were partying, and one of the guys sold some grass to the wrong people. They traced it back to my dorm room. I got caught and got kicked out."

Anton nodded. "Where's Olean?" he asked. Melvin hesitated, then just said, "Upstate, not too far from here."

Anton kept nodding. "Oh, oh, oh, I see, I get it."

As they passed the Harlem Cats corner, Adze said, "College, you and your boyfriend come over here."

Eyes downcast, they complied.

"I have a task for you. It will prove your worthiness to be members of the congregation."

The two said nothing.

"Look across the yard, where the Black Spades hang out. There is an individual there wearing a red bandana. He is in debt to us for some product and is reluctant to pay. I want you two to hurt him bad enough to get the message to pay—and since the two of you are new and only provisional members of our organization here, he probably won't see you coming."

32.

ELMIRA CORRECTIONAL FACILITY, 1979

Heading back from the mess hall a few days later, Melvin led Anton to the tier where the debtor's cell was. Adze was right, he didn't notice them until it was too late. They grabbed him by the legs, tipped him over the second-floor tier and he fell to the concrete floor below busting an arm and some ribs. Anton ran back the way they came and Melvin walked casually the other way. When Anton got to their tier, a guard who saw him running was waiting and slammed him with his baton in the guts, then dragged him off to solitary confinement.

Later, Adze nodded his approval towards Melvin. The red bandana guy couldn't ID Melvin, but the Black Spades started making plans for Anton when he got out of the box. Rumor had it a war was in the making. Negotiations between the factions opened, a compromise was reached and the sharpened toothbrushes, razor whips and bedpost clubs went back to their hiding places. The debt was paid, but Anton was to be left exposed for punishment.

When Anton was out on the yard, the Harlem Cats drove him away from their corner, and the Black Spades all watched him. Anton walked towards the biker corner, and then away when he got close and three of them turned towards him. He then walked towards the weight benches while it was Latino gym class time.

Once again he made a turn when his proximity set off their radar. He kept wandering around the yard, and when back in his cell, spoke to Melvin through his pillow.

"I can't take it, man. They're going to get me sooner or later. They might really fuck me up, even kill me, and Adze and his boys don't give a shit. I do a job for them and they throw me to the wolves. I can't tell the guards, that'd make me a snitch and they'd kill me sure then. I might as well just kill myself and get it over."

"Easy, man, easy. You can survive your time here, you can do it."

"I mean, there's a thousand ways they can get me. A couple of their guys work in the kitchen—they can put something in my food, poison me. When I mop the halls, they got ways to get me there and I'll never see it coming. Out on the yard, you've seen it, it takes the guards time to break up a fight, and these guys got shivs, razors, all kinds of shit, needles with some fucked up disease…"

A week later, somebody started a minor scuffle leaving the mess hall, which drew the guards, and then Anton was surrounded and beaten to a pulp. Before the guards got there, one of Adze's main men, Hammerhead, pulled Anton from the melee and his assailants faded into the crowd. When Anton got out of the infirmary, Adze explained to Anton that Hammerhead was now his protector, and he didn't have to be afraid anymore. However, there was a price to pay, as a similar youth that Hammerhead kept had recently been released.

33.

ELMIRA CORRECTIONAL FACILITY, 1980

Every day, Anton told Melvin of his injuries and humiliation. There were guys who were worse off, who had no protectors, but Melvin noticed Anton looking at the upper tiers as the workmen installed chin link fencing over the top of the handrails on the upper decks, as "falls" were becoming more common.

Although Melvin found himself in the Harlem Cats lowest echelon, Adze had admired how he had disappeared after the red bandana incident, and how on other occasions he had made himself scarce.

"That seems to be a natural skill of yours, College. Making yourself invisible. Yeah, I can see we have a place for you in the organization. You can make things disappear with you, move things around. You can even deliver messages to places me and the other brethren might not be welcome. Yeah. You can ghost it for us, um, huh."

Over the two weeks, Melvin found himself holding a wide assortment of items, contraband drugs, weapons, money, and sometimes verbal messages to "other communities within the institution," as Adze called them.

"Yeah, you're doing good, College. And because you're an educated man, I can be sure you won't fuck up the messages. Yessir, you are proving to be a valuable asset to the Harlem Cats."

When Melvin delivered a message to the Italians about a deal on the outside, he found himself suddenly surrounded. They all smiled at him, and Melvin knew he could be dead before anyone could help, if anyone was going to help. He delivered the message, and the Italians parted, laughing at him as he returned to the Harlem Cats corner of the yard. He also knew that despite his skill at ghosting, he was starting to gain the guards' attention, especially when he drifted over to the white crews. It was just a matter of time before they caught him with some contraband, which would add time to his sentence in this jungle.

"Melvin," Anton whispered one night. Melvin feigned sleep, tired of listening to Anton's whining.

"Melvin!" he said a little louder.

"Keep it down, fool," Melvin answered.

"You see the workmen fencing in the tiers?"

"Yeah."

"They'll be done in a couple of days."

"So?"

"I'm gonna be outta here before they do."

"What?"

"Third tier drop I heard 'em call it."

"What are you talking about, fool?"

"You'll see tomorrow…"

Melvin rolled over with his forearm behind his head and thought.

"Anton… Anton!"

"Yeah?"

"I gotta better idea. Now listen careful…"

The next day in the hallway, Anton picked up a rolled section of the fencing and marched it up to the third tier. Melvin followed at a distance. When he got to the top tier, Anton went to the still open section, dropped the section of fencing and began pulling a bed sheet from under his clothes. Melvin stood several yards down the corridor, fading against the cells. Anton quickly rolled the sheet lengthwise, tied one end to the tier's handrail and the other around his neck. He climbed up on the handrail and holding onto a stanchion was steadying himself in a standing position, when Melvin stepped forward and shouted, "Don't do it, Anton!"

Everyone looked up and saw Anton perched on the railing and Melvin slowly approaching him, his hands held out in supplication. Guards came running.

"Fuck it, man, just fuck it," Anton shouted, shaking his head.

"Yeah, man! Fuck it!" someone shouted from below.

"No, no, man, hold on," Melvin said.

"Fuck it! Fuck it! Fuck it!" The crowd below shouted.

As he heard the guards approaching, Melvin stepped closer and looked at Anton. He saw tears forming on the little man's face. Melvin nodded and rushed forward, grabbing Anton around the waist as he fell forward, eyes closed. Melvin pulled him back onto the tier, holding him tightly and whispering, "What the fuck, man, too damn close," as the guards arrived and seized them both.

34.

ELMIRA CORRECTIONAL FACILITY, 1980

The guards hauled Anton off to the Mental Health Unit, took his clothes, gave him a smock to wear and put him on suicide watch. Melvin got sent back to his cell and was later taken to the psychiatrist's office. The doctor asked him all about Anton, what he'd been doing, what he'd been saying, and then paused and started giving Melvin a real fish-eyed look.

"Are you a friend of Anton's, Melvin?"

"Not really. He got sent here about the same time I did and got the cell next to me. Gotta talk to somebody, you know?"

"You feel sorry for Anton, Melvin? You can see he's gotten knocked around. He says he's gotten into some fights but won't say with whom. You know anything about that?"

"Naw, you know, stuff happens in here."

"The guards are telling me you've been running with the Harlem Cats, maybe moving stuff around for them. Is that true, Melvin?"

"Shit, doc, we just hang out in the same corner of the yard's all."

"Uh huh. When Anton was going to jump, everybody was below, telling him to go ahead. Why did you go up there and help him?"

"He'd been talking funny today, you know? I thought he might have had something going on up there, maybe had some cigarettes or something stashed, see? I went up there to see and holy shit, he's lost it. Dunno what I was thinking, just reacted, that's all."

"Hmm. Says here," the doctor said, opening a file, "that you started college but got kicked out for drugs, right?"

"Yeah, that happened."

"Would you like to try some educational opportunities again, Melvin?"

"Yeah sure, I'd do that."

"They have this program at Fishkill Correctional where you can enroll and start taking college courses as long as you have no disciplinary issues. Since you've served a good portion of your sentence, I think you might be a good candidate for that, Melvin. So far, you have no disciplinary problems listed in your file, and your gang affiliation is listed as 'tentative, to be watched.' If you're interested, I may be able to arrange for a transfer to Fishkill—that's a Medium Security Facility—if you can stay out of trouble."

"Doctor, I think I'd be an ideal candidate for that program. It would be just what I need to help get my life straightened out and back on track. I would not be any kind of troublemaker and would stay away from all the gangs for sure."

Back in his cell, there was another letter from Aunt Erica.

Dear Melvin,

I just finished making a quilt for you and will send it directly. It will keep you warm on these cold winter nights. Your Uncle Bernie and I still have one I made years ago when he was in the army and we love it.

You have been in there for a year and a half now, better than half done if there's no trouble. We pray to the Lord for you every night. Remember what the Psalms say! "I cry to you Lord. I say 'You are my refuge, my portion in the land of the living.

"'Listen to my cry, for I am in desperate need, rescue me from those that pursue me, for they are too strong for me.

"'Set me free from my prison, that I may praise your name;

"'Then the righteous will gather about me because of your goodness to me.'"

Rest assured, Melvin, that we will be here for you. Trust in the Lord and you will make it back to us.

Melvin put the letter down. He hadn't written home but once, asking for some money for his commissary fund. *You're right, Aunt Erica, things are starting to turn around. I will make it out of here.* He finished reading the letter and started to write one back.

The next week two guards showed up in front of his cell. One of the guards said, "Stand up inmate, and face us." When he did, he continued, "Inmate Melvin Peters, you have five minutes to gather your belongings. When you have them together, you will come with us and be transported to the Fishkill Correctional Facility."

Melvin, nodded, sighed and rapidly scooped up all his stuff. He gathered up the letters from Aunt Erica and the quilt and put them on top of the rest. The pictures of the babes on the wall could stay for the next poor slob who got moved into the cell. When he had his gear all together, he looked at the guards and said, "I'm ready, officers."

The guard said into his portable radio, "Open 315."

As they led him down the hallway, Melvin looked into Anton's empty cell. He still was in the Mental Health Unit. *Well, our stunt got him away from Hammerhead and the Harlem Cats,* he thought. *Maybe they'll transfer him to someplace better, too.*

35.

FISHKILL CORRECTIONAL FACILITY, 1980

Melvin applied for the Pell Grant when he got to Fishkill and got assigned to the apprentice program in the cabinetmaking unit as well, where they repaired and refinished government furniture. In the wood shop, the main man was Old Dick, whose gray hair said he'd been there for a long time and his job said he'd behaved himself.

"I probably ain't getting out until I die," he told Melvin as he showed him how to use the different kinds of sandpaper on the desks and cabinets they refinished. "I took an axe to my brother after going on a gin toot. He was looking at my wife," he said, shaking his head.

Melvin learned about dowels and glue, the differences between oak and pine, and Old Dick told him, "You got a short sentence, boy. This is the best place to wait it out. Best place to be if you ain't got a short sentence for that matter." He went silent then, going back to chiseling a cross on a pine casket's lid they had just finished making. Melvin shivered, thinking about being here forever and leaving in a plain pine casket.

36.

LOVEJOY, THE EAST SIDE, 1959

Andy got word of his father's death from the Chojnackis, who lived in the lower flat in the front house. Andy had been paying them to fix his dad's food and clean the cottage. When he pulled up in the driveway, the Chojnacki boy, Chet, was playing with the old man's dog. His mom was standing by the front door of the cottage, her arms crossed. She looked down as she approached Andy, blinking away the tears.

"Andy, I'm so sorry," she said, looking at the ground, sparsely covered with grass.

"He was right there," she said, pointing where Lovejoy's car was. "We heard the dog barking, and when we went to see what it was, he was laying there. We called an ambulance right away..."

"I heard one of them say, 'he's gone' when they picked him up," Chet said.

"Be quiet, Chet! Mr. Rakestraw..."

"It's OK, Mrs. Chojnacki," Andy said.

Mrs. Chojnacki wiped her eyes with a tissue. Andy looked around where the boy was scratching the mutt's head.

"You like the dog, Chet?" he said, thinking the dog looked part beagle and part spaniel.

"He's nice. Sometimes Mr. Rakestraw would let me walk him

when he wasn't feeling good, when he was coughing a lot."

"What's his name, anyway?" Andy said.

"His name's Blaustein. Mr. Rakestraw said he named him after a soldier he was in the army with in World War I. He said Sgt. Blaustein saved his life."

"Well, tell you what Chet," Andy said, peeling a ten out of his money clip. "You take care of Blaustein from now on. Here's some money for his food."

The wide-eyed boy took the money and hugged the dog. Mrs. Chojnacki started to speak, but Andy cut her off.

"I've got to go down to the morgue and claim him. Thanks for everything," and drove away before she could say anything.

Andy went to Meyer Memorial Hospital and claimed the body. He signed the paperwork, called one of T's funeral parlor friends and had the body hauled away and cremated. He never claimed the ashes.

When he went back to empty out the cottage the next day, he looked around at the wobbly used furniture they had lived on for years, smashed it all up and had it hauled away. Except the bed he had slept in, the one that you needed a key to take apart. He's heard that old beds like that were worth money. He continued renting the cottage and stashed weapons he acquired in the walls and under the floor. Remembering his woodshop days in school, he took the old bed apart, sanded it down and stained it. Looking through the yellow pages, he found several antique stores across town on Ashland Street and took the bedstead over there and sold it for twice what he expected. *There's money in this,* he thought. *There's suckers out there who'll pay double, maybe triple what this stuff is worth.* He started going to used furniture stores, picking up solid pieces and fixing them up in the cottage, then selling it to people with no idea of their value.

He took the money and started dressing like the people he sold to, the people who joined country clubs—double-breasted sport coats, Oxford shoes and white shirts open at the neck. Looking the part, he started traveling around the area buying old dressers, chairs and beds being sold off at estate sales. It gave him a charge when he made a sale, knowing he'd gotten over on some college boy businessman or his wife, especially the ones who bragged about how smart they were and how much money they made.

37.

BUFFALO, 1960

Lovejoy had a reputation now, and T used him for murders where discretion was paramount, and especially where bodies needed to vanish. The money came to him in cash and was invested. He purchased the house on Moreland Street, which included the cottage in the back yard. He rented out the front house and kept the cottage for himself. He bought tools and stains, a work table and good camel hair brushes for repairing and refinishing furniture there. He had cards made up, advertising himself as an antiques dealer, and furniture accumulated in the cottage and later in a shop on Ashland Street he rented, then bought, next to the other antique dealers. He stayed in the Hotel Huron downtown, and when T needed him, a message would be left at the desk to "call his cousin." When summoned in this way, he would call Twitch and they would arrange a meeting with T, often in a restaurant out in Batavia near Attica Prison where T liked to take just-released mob members for their first meal out of jail.

38.

THE FIRST WARD, 1960

Andy loved fishing. He had a small runabout that he kept under a pier off South Street on the Buffalo River. When the weather was nice he would hookup an Evinrude outboard and after dodging the ships unloading at the immense grain elevators on the river, motored far out into Lake Erie, away from the industry and the polluted harbor where it was quiet and clean early in the morning. He loved casting a line out and always got a tingle when he got a bite. Then came the battle of wits with the fish. The smallmouth bass were fun and tricky.

He saved his money and bought bigger reels and more lures so he could go out further to catch walleye. He learned the walleye were best sought in about fifty feet of water, which took him way out in the lake. Andy figured about a 6 oz. sinker was best and varied between his spinners and spoons for lures, then watched the new Whirlaway reel as it passed about ten times letting out about 200' of line, putting the lure far away and deep where the fish wouldn't suspect a thing. He would troll along, watching the water, knowing his prey would snag the lure eventually. Other fishermen in cabin cruisers shook their head when they saw him out there in his little boat, not afraid of sudden weather changes or distance from the shore.

How big are you? he thought when he snagged one. *How should I play this one? He's strong, I'll have to let out line and play him.* He saw the other fishermen out there in their Chris Crafts and thought, *Someday, a few more jobs and I'll have a boat like yours.* Then he could really go after the biggest fish in the lake, the muskies. He knew he'd catch the real monsters then.

39.

LACKAWANNA, NY, 1964

T summoned him, but this time it wasn't to the restaurant in Batavia. Lovejoy met him in Lackawanna Stadium. He walked past the purple Cadillac in the parking lot and was surprised to see Twitch still behind the wheel. The grass on the field was burned and spotty and the paint on the concrete stands chipped and faded. Walking around the playing field, he saw T seated halfway up on the concrete benches, watching him through sunglasses. He stiffened a little and hesitated, looked around, but saw they were alone. *You never can tell with these guys,* he thought. T continued to stare as he approached up the steps, *like Ben Hur meeting the emperor in the movie,* he thought. He walked up a couple of rows below T, then stopped. Sitting down, he relaxed.

"I have a job for you, Lovejoy," he said. "It's important and must be done very carefully." He paused, and Lovejoy nodded silently. "No one besides me and you in Buffalo will know about it." Another pause. "We are doing this for a friend, out of town." More silence. "It will show the power of our arm. Our reach," he said, raising his hand in a fist. "There is a trouble maker, a *mooli*, who is causing problems for our friend's business in a town along the Hudson River." T took an envelope out of his suit pocket and handed it to Lovejoy. "Here is information about him. It doesn't matter if he is found or not. Just make him go away."

Lovejoy scanned the newspaper articles in the envelope about a civil rights activist in the town along the Hudson. One article said the man was making the local government agencies jump, lately getting them to make improvements to schools and garbage pick-ups in the Black neighborhood. His civic association was called "Free at Last," and there was a picture of him with Martin Luther King, Jr. In another article, the activist, Joshua Lowe, complained about gambling and loan sharking controlled by out-of-town interests and called for state prosecutors to look into it and possible local corruption. He was running for a position as a State Assemblyman and expected to win.

"When does it have to be done?" Lovejoy asked.

"Soon. Before he wrecks our friend's business."

"Won't his death bring attention?"

T turned to him and the sunglasses came off. "That's not your problem."

The wheels were turning in Lovejoy's head. "I'll need a car."

"It will be ready."

Lovejoy got up to leave.

"You will be rewarded well for this," T said, and it made Lovejoy think of the boats he had seen in the armory show.

A trip to the library and a look at the town newspapers told Lovejoy about this Joshua Lowe and his habitat. The Black people lived mostly north of the downtown, and the men there mostly worked at big commercial laundries, a wallpaper manufactory and a gypsum plant. Recently, local bookmaking operations in the plants had been broken up by the police and Lowe was calling for investigations into outside interests controlling vice in the area.

Lovejoy drove out to the small city that seemed to be built into the rock cliffside along the Hudson, and after a few passes along the river he headed inland through the downtown and headed north, past the Civil War monument into a Black neighborhood on a dimly lit street. There he found his target's political headquarters on the first floor of a four-story red brick building that had seen better days. A hand painted wooden sign reading, *Free at Last* hung out over the sidewalk. A couple of blocks up the street he located the outfit's unofficial headquarters, a bar and restaurant called The Black Duck in a brick storefront built onto the front of a big wooden house. Out front, there was a sign with an image of a ferocious Daffy Duck with a baseball bat on his shoulder. Driving back along the river he found several piers, once active with tankers in the wintertime, but now unused except by fishermen. Getting out his pole, he did some casting, and found out from local anglers the area was good for brown trout, and that striped bass were the best sportfish in that part of the river, giving even more fight than salmon. They also told him herring was the best bait to use and where to rent boats.

Lovejoy examined the route between the Free at Last office and the bar where Lowe hung out. Lowe usually left the office around five and headed up to The Black Duck, usually with a couple of associates. Lovejoy smiled when he saw crews in hard hats throwing up construction barriers out in front of the bar to repair the sewerage lines, and read in the local papers that Lowe's complaints about sewage backing up in nearby houses had made it happen. *Be careful what you wish for,* he thought.

Joshua Lowe hung up the phone and raising his fist in the air, shouted "Yes!"

Everyone in the office looked at him, and he said, "Ladies and gentlemen, *The Evening Star* says I've got a 65 % rating in the latest poll. Next stop Albany!"

A cheer went up, and one worker shouted from his desk, "Hey man, that calls for a celebration!"

"I'd say it does, I'd say it does, my friends," Lowe said. "And, since it's getting on in the evening, why don't we all head on down to the Duck and I'll buy the first round."

That statement was met with agreement, and the campaign crew started putting away papers and files, and gathering coats and hats.

Lovejoy's watch said 4:15, and the news said sundown was at 4:25 that evening. Lovejoy washed his face and dressed in clothes he'd bought en route at the Goodwill in Weedsport. He went out to the parking lot of the motel, and after checking to make sure no one was watching, moved a double-barreled shotgun, a .38 pistol and ski mask from the trunk onto the car seat next to him, and covered it all up with a blanket. Going into town, he drove slowly down the street past the Free at Last office, past the bar, parked and slid down in the seat to wait in the darkness. Lowe and the others left the office a little after five and drove off towards the bar. Unable to park with the construction crew's obstructions, they went past Lovejoy looking for a parking spot.

When Lowe found one a block from the bar on the right side of the street, Lovejoy put on the ski mask, rolled down the passenger side window and, propping the barrel of the shotgun on the window sill, drove up just as Lowe was getting out of his car. Lowe looked up, saw the ski masked man aiming the shotgun and tried to run. Lovejoy gunned the engine and smashed Lowe into the car door and took it off the hinges.

"Motherfucker!" shouted Lowe's friend, getting out on the passenger side. Lovejoy fired the shotgun and the man flew back, grabbing his face. Another man getting out of the back seat ducked as Lovejoy drove forward, crushing Lowe and the door on the pavement. He backed up and fired the shotgun's other barrel, keeping the witness on the sidewalk. He then picked up the pistol, drove forward, veering left to avoid the victim and the car door, opened his passenger door and shot Lowe twice more.

He sped off, the door swinging inward as he went. A quick look in the rear-view mirror revealed people coming out on the sidewalk and shouting. He stopped, pulled the passenger door completely shut, then fired blindly back down the street out the window, sending the curious and the concerned diving for cover. Hitting the gas, he left town on a route along back roads he had mapped in his head that led to a wooded spot along the river. He pulled over, shut off his lights and tossed both weapons far out into the rapidly moving stream. Through the trees, he saw the flashing red and blue lights and heard the sirens of the police speeding by. His spine tingled at how close they'd come, how he'd outsmarted his pursuers. *Right according to plan,* he thought. *They'll be one step behind me all the way.*

Farther up river, he changed clothes and deposited the Goodwill rags with the ski mask in a shopping bag weighted with a few bricks and dropped them into the river. Still farther up the Hudson, he drove out onto one of the unused piers where he'd been fishing and rolled all the windows down. Taking a deep breath, he opened the car door, hit the gas, rolled out himself onto the pier, then watched as the car had just enough momentum to go over the edge into the river. *Yes!* he thought, watching as the sedan bobbed for a while, drifted in the current and sank away from the pier. He looked around, listened, stood up and dusted himself off. *Perfect,* he thought. *No evidence left at all.* He walked a short distance to where he had parked his blue Mercury and drove towards the bridge heading west across the river. His skin felt electrified when he spotted the state troopers before the toll stop to the bridge. A tall policeman in a gray uniform and a Stetson hat shone a light into his car and looked around.

"Please step out of the car, sir," he said, his eyes on Lovejoy and his free hand near his sidearm.

"Sure, officer. Is something wrong?" he said, handing his license to a second trooper.

"Step away from the car please," and a third trooper approached and began looking inside his car, opening the glove box and reaching under the seats.

"Can you open the trunk please?"

"OK. Sure. What's this about anyway?"

The troopers didn't respond. Lovejoy took his keys and opened the trunk. The first trooper flashed his light within, spotting wet fishing gear and an ice chest. He opened the ice chest where there were three trout iced down and two beer cans on top.

"Just trout, officers. Couldn't manage any stripers. And I keep the beer in the back, too, officer. I wouldn't drink while I was driving."

The trooper closed the trunk and waved to the others at the roadblock.

"You can go, sir," he said, and Lovejoy smiled as he got back into the car. *One step ahead of you all the way, dummies,* he thought as he gave the toll taker a quarter.

Lovejoy was driving west on the thruway, ready to gloat when he went back to Buffalo. He knew Twitch would deliver his "lunch," look inside the package and see all the money. Stopping in a diner along the lake near Syracuse, Lovejoy saw on the eleven o'clock news that Lowe was dead, his friend was blinded but alive, and police were seeking a man in an older maroon sedan. Lovejoy sipped coffee and ordered dessert, thinking his timing was right, that buying a boat was cheapest in the fall and winter.

40.

DOWNTOWN BUFFALO, 1965

Whenever there was an out-of-town job to be done, T spoke directly to Lovejoy now, and never told Strazzo, Squalo or any of the others about it. *That way,* T thought, *I've always got something in my back pocket in case someone thinks about betraying me.* Strazzo and Squalo were the closest to him in the family, had their own crews by this time and were always trying to one up each other. *Time to organize the empire,* he thought, *like the Romans would do in the old days with their provinces.*

T met the two underbosses in the back room of the old restaurant on the Terrace downtown. The two men were wearing their best suits and sat silently through the antipasto. T ordered dinner for all three of them. When their meals arrived, Strazzo and Squalo listened.

"It took a long time to build up our business here," T said. "The construction, the union, the gambling." Both underbosses nodded and ate. "We need to keep it organized, not trip over each other. From now on, Grant, you'll be the union man, the construction man. Ralph, you stay closest to the neighborhood. You take care of the games, the betting, the loans."

Both underlings nodded, then Squalo put down his fork, hesitated and said, "What about my job in the union?" T watched him close his fists. Strazzo had the beginning of a smile, thinking of a friend who wanted that job.

"Grant runs everything there. He decides who gets the jobs. You run the games. There will be no arguments."

The rest of the meal was silent, with Squalo barely touching the salad at the end, calculating the loss of the no-show business agent's job with the laborer's union. *That's forty grand a year!* he thought, *and four or five more in expenses. And the use of the friggin' Lincoln, too!* Eager to leave, he thought of the Thursday night Ziginat game down at the social club, when he'd tell Strazzo's boys they no longer got a cut of the action, and that he'd be making all the loans there from now on. He thought of the bookies he'd summon to the café and tell them from now on all the take came back to him. *Screw me out of the union job, will you?* he thought.

Finally, the meal was over. As both underbosses got up to leave, T said, tapping his index finger on the table, "Remember, my cut remains the same. *Per sempre.*"

Out in the parking lot, Squalo slammed the door on his plum Coupe de Ville and thought, *The old man never said anything about the dope. Open territory since we got rid of that Canuck bastard. Time to make it all mine before that prick moves in.*

41.

LAKE CAYUGA, NY, 1970

Every Friday, Linda met her husband Tim after work at the bar with the knotty pine paneling. The local real estate market was tough.

"So, Tim, how did you do with the guy over on Frontenac?" she said, as he brought their beers over to the table near the window where they could look out through the trees and see the wind rippling the water on Lake Cayuga.

Tim paused a moment staring at his beer stein on the varnished blonde table, and said, "OK. Good. He's going to buy the place. Said he actually liked the narrow windows, didn't complain about the long driveway to the road either."

"Well, that's good, right? He's not knocking the price down so far you won't make any money, is he?"

Taking a slow swig of beer, Tim shook his head and said, "Naw, he took it down some, but we'll be OK there. The way he looked the place over was a little weird, is all."

"Hmmm," Linda said smiling. "Is he thinking of opening up a whore house or something?"

"No, nothing like that. It was eerie, though, the way he walked around the outside of the house and, a couple of times, pointed and swept his arm about forty-five degrees back and forth."

She knew Tim was having trouble adjusting from the Army. "I wonder what that was about?"

Tim shook his head again. "It was the same moves my platoon sergeant used to make when we'd set up in-country. He's look around, do that same motion and place our fighting holes and the M-60 that way."

"Huh."

"Then he asked me if I knew any landscapers. Said if he bought the house, he wanted to take out all the trees and bushes around the place for fifty feet."

"I wonder why he would want to get rid of all that shade?"

"Dunno, but fifty feet's beyond any accurate range for a pistol…"

"What's this guy do, anyway?"

"Antiques dealer. Said he'd found this place when he was out here checking out estate sales. Credit report's solid."

"Well, that's good, too. You thought nobody was going to buy that place, now you can put it out of your mind. Say, how about we stay here at the Pines for the fish fry tonight?" she said.

42.

TRUMANSBURG, NY, 1972

The only person in Buffalo who knew where Lovejoy lived out on the Finger Lakes was T. As T got older, Twitch watched his boss more carefully and noticed that he started to get names wrong, forget phone numbers. T would shake his head, tap his temple and pat Twitch on the shoulder on those occasions. When the numbers came to him, Twitch wrote them down in a small notebook he made up for him and made a copy for himself. Twitch would watch him when he took it out. After a meeting in Batavia with T and Lovejoy, Twitch followed Lovejoy back to Trumansburg, trailing behind him on the country roads, then watching from the woods as the killer went up the long drive to the house in the clearing. For everybody else, Lovejoy was just a whispered name.

Lovejoy loved his place on the Finger Lakes, away from the soot and grime of Buffalo and in the center of some of the best fishing in the country. When he'd settled into the house by Lake Cayuga, he got a runabout to catch the trout and largemouth bass on the lake and would travel all around the area to go fishing. The muskies were becoming fewer in Lake Erie but he still liked going out on the lake and showing off his cabin cruiser. He never joined a boat club but enjoyed going to them to find vulnerable women in the bars and wives feuding with their yachtsmen husbands. He discovered salmon and steelhead trout were good sport in the Salmon River in Tug Hill.

Then there was the northern pike. When Lovejoy found out they were territorial and didn't just strike when they were hungry, he started buying different lures for them and mapping out places in the Adirondacks to catch the aggressive fish. They toyed with the bait sometimes before they struck, and when Lovejoy felt the would-be killer's tapping on the bait, he'd start reeling faster, knowing the lure's quick movement told the pike his would-be prey was panicking and in peril.

When the weather got cold, Lovejoy would go skiing, traveling around the northeast getting a rush speeding downhill and around trees on the steepest slopes. The lounges at the resorts were good hunting grounds as well, and Andy, the antique dealer from Western New York, never left a trail for any woman to follow him back home to the Finger Lakes.

Lovejoy followed the New York and Buffalo papers from his house in Trumansburg. When he read of numerous mob-related shootings and of the kidnapping of one of T's cousins in New York, he called the Jersey Street Café and asked for T from a gas station out on Route 96. The people who worked at the café knew the usual coded answer was to say, "He's in the john," after which a ritual of movement to an untapped phone would ensue. This time was different, though.

"He's not here now," the manager answered.

Lovejoy looked at his watch and thought, *He's always there for coffee at this time.* Several more phone calls around Buffalo revealed that T, Squalo, Strazzo and several others were not anywhere to be found in their usual places. *Something bad is happening between these guys,* he thought, *and getting in the middle of it is not a good idea.* He looked out the kitchen window at the snow falling and figured it might be time to get out of town, and not just a ski resort. Time to get way out of town, and he put a call in to a travel agent in Syracuse that specialized in cruises to Europe.

On the first day on the *S.S. Rotterdam*, Lovejoy saw giggling college girls, strutting divorcees and timid schoolteachers along the teak decks of the ship. He took a swim in the indoor pool and watched all the women in swimsuits there. He did the sauna next, relaxing on a redwood chaise lounge with his eyes just open enough to see. Then came the Captain's lounge, with blue carpets, gold leather chairs and sunset lighting. He ordered a Crown Royal on the rocks and started sizing up the prospects. Couples sitting at the low marble topped tables he barely noticed until he spotted one pair who never seemed to speak. She had short dark hair and he'd noticed that by the pool she'd worn a black one-piece suit that fit her like paint. Even in the bar's dimmed lighting she hid behind large round sunglasses. The man had tinted aviator glasses and his sculptured short blonde hair said money. They never looked at each other, never smiled and walking past he heard them speaking both French and English. *Perfect,* he thought. *That type loves to play games, and when the cruise is over, it'll be goodbye.*

The third afternoon out of port, the brunette was pulling one strap of her bathing suit over her shoulder while Lovejoy lay back on the bed, listening to her Quebecois accent.

"He wants to divorce me, you know," she said.

"You'll be pretty well off, I'm sure," Andy the American antiques dealer said.

"Not as much as it would be if he were dead, the pig." She bent down against him. "Do you know anyone who might do such a thing? Some mafia friends you might have in New York?"

Aroused, he thought, *You have no idea.* He thought about the possibilities, the money she had told him her husband was worth. The trouble in the mob back home. Life with her in Europe. Push him over the side, nobody would ever find him. Take him out after they arrived in LeHarve... *No, that's crazy. No way you could trust this broad. Somebody probably saw us together. How would I get this done in France? It's not Buffalo or New York where I could get weapons, cars, know the streets.*

Putting his hands behind his head he said, "I'm just a business man on a cruise, baby, I don't know any bad guys like that."

She stood up and pulled the other strap up over her shoulder.

43.

UNIVERSITY HEIGHTS, NORTH BUFFALO, 1980

When Leo came in from the backyard and put the platter of grilled lamb chops on the table, the three children sat around the dining room table. Adele and Cecile brought in bowls of vegetables and boiled potatoes from the kitchen. The smell of the still sizzling chops wafting through the room, Leo sat down at the head of the table.

"Jimmy," Dunleavy said, "please say grace."

"In the name of the Father and the Son and the Holy Spirit," Jimmy began, then rushed through the prayer. Once finished, he reached over and grabbed the biggest chop.

"Gees, Jimmy, don't be so grabby," his younger sister Bridget said.

"He's a hungry boy," Leo said, passing a bowl of peas.

"Mind your manners, anyway, Jimmy, this isn't feeding time at the zoo," Adele added.

As the food was passed around, Cecile swung her straight brown hair back over her shoulder and to Adele's approval, used the serving fork to get a chop.

"Well, Cecile, what did you learn in your classes today?" Leo said.

"We're reading Dostoyevsky's *Crime and Punishment* now, Dad."

"Oh, and what class is that in?"

"It's a famous novel by Dostoyevsky, Dad," Jimmy said between mouthfuls. Adele gave him a frown.

"It's in English class, Dad. There's a student named Raskolnikov who believes that the end justifies the means. He kills a nasty old pawnbroker because he needs the money to keep his sister from marrying an old rich guy for the money so he can go to school. He thinks he's got 'the right to transgress' because he's special and will do the world good in the long run, and society's a better place without the greedy old lady. But Raskolnikov's conscience bothers him, and there's this magistrate who knows he did it." She paused to take a small bite.

Leo swallowed, then said, "It sounds kind of like the guy in Edgar Allen Poe's 'The Telltale Heart.' His conscience gets to him."

"Well, yeah, kinda," Cecile said, "but there's more to it. It discusses utilitarian morality, the sublimating of conscience. It get really deep into ethics."

"Well, this Raskinov... Raskolnikov, is that it? He's a criminal, a murderer, right?"

"Yes, he kills the pawnbroker, and her sister who witnesses the murder."

"A no good killer. No way to justify a double homicide. And how does the policeman, or magistrate, get him?"

Cecile smiled. "He works on Raskolnikov's conscience, Dad. He keeps after him... like you would."

Leo nodded. Staring ahead, he said, "Sometimes that's not enough. It's not that easy. Some people don't have any conscience."

Adele gave him a look. *Something's bugging him,* she thought.

44.

NIAGARA FALLS, 1980

Squalo barely had the car in park before his grandkids, Tony and Terri had jumped out and were running towards the aquarium entrance.

"Hey! Watch out for cars!" he shouted, heaving himself out of the front seat.

"Are we on time for the show?" Tony, age eight, said, racing up the stairs.

"Yeah! Yeah! Grandpa! Are we on time to see the dolphin show?" Terri, age six said.

"Yeah, kids, we'll be on time for the first show, just let grandpa buy the tickets."

While Squalo bought the tickets, the two children raced around the hall, looking at the fish exhibits.

"Look at the pretty fish colors!" Terri said, watching clownfish swim in and out of the coral.

"What's that stuff? The green and blue and yellow plants?" Tony said.

"That's coral," said a guide. "It's actually thousands of little animals growing together."

"All those different colors!" Terri said.

"OK, kids, let's see the dolphin show!" Squalo said, herding the two children into the auditorium, where they looked down on a pool where staff members in wet suits assembled hoops and buckets of fish while dolphins swam in circles around the pool.

"There they are Grandpa!" Terri said.

When the crowd had settled in, the show began, with the dolphins slapping their fins against staff members' hands, leaping through hoops and walking backwards across the surface of the pool. The kids watched and cheered while Squalo looked at the female attendant in the skin tight wet suit.

After the show, they went through the other exhibits and Squalo stopped them in front of the shark tank as the swift killers slid through the water, their small black eyes alert and mouth set. Squalo tried to pull his lips back the same way.

"*Annnh*, he's scary looking," Terri said as one shark came close to the glass enclosure then darted away just before making contact.

"He could kill any of these other fish, whenever he wanted," Squalo said.

Terri shivered. "Let's go over here, grandpa," she said, trying to pull him by hand towards the seal exhibit.

"Go ahead, kids, Grandpa wants to see these guys."

The children went to the seal exhibit, where a guide explained that the Niagara Falls Aquarium was one of the first to establish a rescue facility for blind and injured seals and sea lions, pointing out one seal missing a fin.

"Awww," Terri said. Tony took her hand.

Squalo turned to a guide while the sharks swiftly changed directions, avoiding collisions with one another.

"Hey, these sharks, whaddaya call them?"

"Those are blacktip reef sharks. They're common to the waters around…"

"These guys always this ready to go like that? They ever go after each other?"

"No. In the wild they only go after smaller fish and that's what we feed them here."

"Ever put 'em in with the other fish? What would happen then?"

"No, that wouldn't work very well, sir. The other fish would try to hide, but in the limited space we have, they couldn't survive."

"Scare the hell out of 'em, then eat 'em." Squalo said, smiling. "They never fight or kill each other, huh? Show each other who's boss?"

"Not that I've observed or heard about, sir."

"Huh," Squalo said and went to catch up to his grandchildren.

45.

UNIVERSITY HEIGHTS, NORTH BUFFALO, 1980

Leo came into the house whistling after work, kissed Adele in the kitchen, hung up his coat, looked around to find Bridget and Jimmy watching *The Towering Inferno* on TV, and Cecile reading in the living room.

"Studying?" Leo asked.

"Um hmm," she answered.

"What are you reading now?" Leo said.

"About the Knapp Commission in New York. Do you know much about it, Dad?" she said.

"Yes, some. A bad business. What subject is that for?" Leo said.

"Urban American History. We have to write a paper on the operation of a department of the city government. I picked the police department," she said, looking up at him and smiling.

"Oh, I see. Do you need any help?" Leo said.

"Uh, not right now. I've got these books," she said, picking up two off the couch. *Varieties of Police Behavior*, by James Q. Wilson and *The Knapp Commission Report*.

"Well, if you need some help, I haven't read many books about urban history, but I can tell you how police departments operate," he offered, looking over the books she had handed him.

"Dad," she said, looking down, "my teacher, Mr. Roberts, and a lot of the kids in class think policemen are lazy and racist. And he says a lot of them are crooked."

There was a long pause. Roberts, he thought. "Is that Harold Roberts you're talking about, Ceelee?" *H.R., he called himself back then. The S.O.B. radical we had trouble with ten years ago on the U.B. campus.*

"Did you know of any cop... I mean policemen, like that?" she said.

Leo let out a long breath. "Like in any profession, Ceelee, there are people who are bad, and the police are no exceptions. Some are lazy and cut corners, and some steal. In the old days, when I was a rookie, I worked a case..."

"Dinner's ready!" Adele announced from the kitchen.

During dinner, Adele noticed that Leo was strangely silent, instead of asking about what the kids had been doing like he usually did. Jimmy talked about going out for the basketball team.

Leo thought about his first plainclothes work, almost thirty years ago. He was a rookie walking a beat and nobody outside his neighborhood and precinct in South Buffalo knew him. The Commissioner's Confidential Squad used him to watch out for patrolmen on the take, accepting payoffs for illegal pinball machines used for gambling. "Wear whatever you do when you go out with the guys," Inspector Wachter had said. How innocent it all seemed now, with drugs and the utter ruthlessness that had brought. He shivered, thinking about the mutilated burned body of a drug dealing Canadian found in a field back in the 60s...

"And was Melissa at the dance?" Bridget asked Jimmy.

"Uh, yeah, she was there."

"Did you dance with her?" Adele asked.

Jimmy squirmed. Leo smiled, but kept silent, knowing girlfriends were the last thing the boy wanted to talk about in front of the family.

46.

ALLENTOWN, THE WEST SIDE, 1980

Twitch walked down to the end of Allen Street at Day's Park. A man stood shivering at the edge of the park, watching his dog sniff the ground. "C'mon, c'mon, Pollock. Take a dump and let's get inside," he muttered as Twitch walked around the dry cleaners on the corner and down the alley until he was behind the recently closed bar. Looking up and down the alley, he then walked to the saloon's back door, which he nudged open with the toe of his worn-out sneaker. Once inside, he coughed loudly and listened. *Nothing,* he thought. He pulled a flashlight out of his pocket and played it around the room. Empty bottles littered the bar. Looking over the bar, Twitch saw the sinks pulled away from the bar and pipes missing. A look in the bathrooms showed the copper and galvanized pipe torn out there, too. *Just right, the junkies have been at work for a while.*

He took a crowbar from under his coat and ripped away some of the paneling from the walls, exposing the channels to the second floor. Opening the hatch behind the bar to the basement, he stomped on the stairs and heard the rats scurrying away below. Testing each step as he descended, he carefully moved to the wall where the fuse box was, pulled the main breaker and began stripping the insulation from the wires heading up the wall, then wrapped the wires in newspaper. He repeated the process on the first and second floor, then went into the kitchen and opened the drain on the deep fat fryer, causing the rancid grease to leak slowly onto the floor. He shut down the gas to the stove, then tore out some of the gas pipes, took a deep breath and ripped out the live gas line to the fryer. Moving quickly, he went back into the basement, turned the electricity back on and left the way he had come in, closing the back door quietly.

"Use your head, not gasoline," Sammy had told him. "The firemen and the cops can smell it a mile away, and then the insurance company'll laugh at you when you say, 'Where's my money?' Oh yeah, make sure you've sent letters to Niagara Mohawk to show you told 'em to shut off the electric and the gas. It'll take weeks for them to get around to, and in the meantime, all kinds of accidents can happen in empty houses. Do it right and they'll pay off and you're rid of some dump in a neighborhood that's going down." Twitch thought of this as he got into his car and took a deep breath. He reached into his pants pocket for his keys, stopped, then patted down the other pockets. The flashlight. He'd left it behind. Too late now, the joint's filling up with gas. Shit. Hell, it'll get burned up when the place takes off.

47.

UNIVERSITY HEIGHTS, NORTH BUFFALO, 1980

Leo Dunleavy was watching the Sabres game, and Jerry Korab had just slammed Bryan Trottier into the boards. "That's it, Jerry, check the man and the puck comes loose," he said.

Adele looked over the top of her *Time* magazine and asked, "He can check, but can he skate?"

The scanner next to the pile of magazines on the stand between them beeped. "An alarm of fire, 251 Allen Street, Box 2165. Engines 2, 37 and 16, Ladders 9 and 4, Battalion 4 respond for the report of smoke coming from the building, 2340 hours."

"Huh," Leo said, as Jim Schoenfeld snagged Danny Gare's pass and wristed it over Billy Smith's shoulder.

Adele looked at Leo closely, the smoke from her Tareyton 100 drifting upward. "That's an understatement from you," she said.

"No, no, it was a great play. It's just that one of T's joints is on fire. Closed a little while ago, too. I'll bet one of his boys lit it off."

Adele stared at the ceiling and shook her head.

Captain Paul Calabotta stood up when two bells sounded but kept his eye on the TV as Gare passed the puck to Schoenfeld. When one bell trilled after a pause, he said, "Gotta be us, boys," and started backing up towards the engine room, eyes still on the hockey game, as the other firemen got out of their lounge chairs in the day room. The next set of six bells were striking when Schoenfeld's wrist shot beat the goalie and Rick Jenerette was shouting "He scores!" from the press box as they were kicking off their shoes and donning boots. The last set of five bells was just finishing as the loudspeaker began to announce the address. Calabotta jumped up in the front seat, heard both the pumper's doors slam behind him and the diesel roar into life as he repeated, "251 Allen" to Fahey, the driver who sat next to him.

"Hydrant's just over on College," Fahey said, cranking the steering wheel as the Ward LaFrance pumper bumped down the apron and turned onto the street. Calabotta's foot pounded the siren button on the floor while he buckled his coat with one hand and keyed the radio mic with the other. "Engine 2 responding."

Calabotta tightened the straps to his air pack as they roared up Wadsworth, the engine's red lights reflecting off the windows on the wooden houses. Sniffing the smoky air, Fahey said, "It's off," as Calabotta rapped on the window separating them from the rear compartment where the two firefighters sat, donning their gear. He nodded at the two men, then looked forward as they pulled onto Allen, observing the gray smoke pushing out of the seams of the building and rising from the cellar hatch in the sidewalk. *Shit, a basement fire.*

"Engine 2 on location, we've got a two-story brick structure with smoke showing, holding all units," he said on the radio. Then to Fahey, "We'll stretch the deuce and half, Pat, fire's cranking in the basement." Fahey nodded as the two firefighters got off the rig, and when he saw Aaron and Tuzinski shoulder the heavy brass nozzle and four sections of the hose, drove off to connect to the hydrant up the street, the heavy fabric hose flopping off the truck onto the street as he went.

Calabotta led the two firemen over the sidewalk and knelt down to the right of the bar's front door with the others to put their masks on.

"It's in the basement, men. Good thing I know this saloon," he chuckled, pulling his rubber boots all the way up. He stood and jammed the forks of his Halligan bar into the door jamb just below the lock and pried it outward. The old wooden door cracked apart and came open, hot brown smoke instantly enveloping them.

Sticking his masked face next to the young nozzleman, Calabotta said, "Follow me to the left, Aaron. We'll crawl to the hatch behind the bar and blast it once I get it open. Then follow me down the steps quick and we'll kill it in the basement."

They crawled inside the bar, the captain swinging the Halligan bar back and forth in front of him. *Might be some bum passed out on the floor.* Feeling the heat penetrating his rubber boots, he thought, *Gotta hit it quick before it gets away from us,* and scrambled forward, finding the opening at the bar and feeling for the hatch. Finding the ring to open it, he turned once more to the nozzleman and shouted, "Ready?" and as he pulled on the hatch door, the hundred-year-old timbers holding the floor up gave way, tumbling Calabotta and Aaron into the inferno below.

48.

When Dunleavy entered the hospital room, there were two people present, and neither one of them was moving. Firefighter Aaron Jefferson lay still on the bed, his arms and most of his head swathed in white bandages. There was a green plastic mask over his mouth and nose feeding him oxygen, and the black skin of his face that wasn't covered with bandages was blistered and smeared with white cream. A monitor beeped out his pulse rate and a green line depicting his heart rhythm jogged across another screen. The other man in the room was seated next to the bed. He must have weighed over 300 pounds, his legs were ready to bust out of the jeans he wore, and his football lineman arms emerged from a short-sleeved blue T-shirt with a Maltese cross that read "Ladder 9". His face had blisters also, covered with the white ointment along his jawline, and his short dark hair was singed in places.

Dunleavy reached out to the silent giant. The fireman took his hand and said quietly, "Zeke, Ladder 9."

"Leo Dunleavy, Homicide. Can you talk about it, son?"

The big man nodded. "Yes."

"Just tell me what happened."

Zeke hesitated, shook his head, cleared his throat and began. "We pulled up right behind the engine. When Fahey took off for the hydrant, we moved up right in front of the building. 2's crew popped the door and went in while we were getting off the rig. I followed the hose line in... and they dropped out of sight into the cellar."

He hesitated, then continued. "I snagged Tuzinski just as he was falling into the hole and yanked him back. We both reached down, trying to grab Jefferson and the Captain. Then we grabbed a ladder and shoved it down into the hole, and Tuzinski and 37's crew stretched another hoseline to cover us... I grabbed the kid here first," he said, gesturing with his chin, "and hauled him up the ladder. When the guys up top snatched him, I went back down and got Captain Calabotta... his mask had gotten knocked off... I just grabbed him and went straight up... he was, he was..." and he dropped his head on his chest, his hands on his knees.

Dunleavy patted the fireman on the shoulder. Dunleavy's hand came away wet, and he realized there must be more of the burn cream on his shoulders too. "You did all you could, fireman. Have you spoken to the arson detectives yet?"

Zeke nodded.

"OK. We'll talk later, Zeke. If you think of anything, give myself or any of my detectives a call," he said, leaving a card on a table there.

"Get these motherfuckers, Lieutenant. Get them and string them up," Zeke said with tears in his eyes.

As Dunleavy left, several other firemen were coming in to see their burned brother. One said, "Some guys are talking getting the Union to post a reward to help catch the guy who did this."

"Probably some Allentown junkie did it," another said.

49.

BUFFALO FIREFIGHTERS' UNION HALL, 1980

Three days after the fire killed Captain Calabotta, the Firefighters' Union had a special meeting. Zeke arrived early, sat dead center in the front row and waited for the President to call for new business. When he did, Zeke stood up and faced his fellow firefighters. The rookies in the crowd stared at the blisters on his face, and his hair was trimmed to a brush cut.

"You guys all know what happened to me. You guys all know Jefferson and knew Captain Calabotta. I want to make a motion that we put together a reward of ten grand for the capture and conviction of the bastard who started that fire on Allen, and I'm putting two grand of my own money towards it."

"I'll second that!" shouted several members.

"They oughta just turn the S.O.B. over to us when they catch him!" shouted another, and several others yelled what they'd like to do to the arsonist.

"All right, all right, take it easy. We've got a motion on the floor to set up a $10,000 reward for the capture and conviction…"

"Or death!" shouted a fireman.

"…of the arsonist who set the fire that killed Cap Calabotta and burned Aaron and Zeke. The motion has been seconded. All those in favor…"

He didn't finish the sentence when "Aye!" was shouted by everyone in the room.

"All right. The motion passes. Zeke, you and I are going to make the rounds of the TV stations, the radio stations and the newspapers to get the word out about this reward."

By the time the meeting had ended, all ten thousand had been pledged and the membership was ready to start searching the streets for the arsonist. Several bar fights erupted as alcohol fueled firemen spread across the city after the meeting in a rage and only understanding policemen kept a few from winding up in jail themselves.

50.

BUFFALO POLICE HEADQUARTERS, 1980

Dunleavy went up to the Arson Squad office on the 3rd floor of police headquarters and was waved into the commander's office, where the unit commander, Keith MacIntyre, was huddling with three other policemen, two wearing blue coveralls and smelling of smoke, and the other one in his shirtsleeves and tie.

"C'mon in, Chief," MacIntyre said.

"Gentlemen," Dunleavy said, nodding. "I hear you've got something for me."

"We do, Chief. We've officially classified the fire only as 'suspicious' so far, but we found a couple of interesting items," he said, holding up two plastic bags. "This," he said, raising one holding a flashlight, "we found by the back door, which was open. There are several partial prints on it, which we asked the identification bureau to rush through. We're waiting right now for the results, expected any time now. The second item," he said, holding up the other bag, "is dog shit."

"Dog shit?" Dunleavy said.

"Yup, dog shit. Medium size dog, we figured. I had detective Asciutto here," he said, nodding towards a big man with bushy hair and a mustache standing to his right, "keep an eye on the alley out back, ask around and find the dog who left this," shaking the bag. "We thought the owner might have seen something, as frequently as his dog goes there. Kevin, tell Chief Dunleavy what you discovered."

The mustached detective cleared his throat and smiled. "It only took a few hours to find the owners—of the shit and the dog," and they all chuckled. "Lives over on Days Park. The night of the fire, he did walk his dog, and he did see someone in the alley—a nervous, white male who he described as all 'herky jerky.'"

"Did you say herky jerky?" Dunleavy said.

"Yes sir. The man said he saw a skinny, white guy, around fifty years old."

"Fellas, if my hunch is right, we should start prepping an interrogation room..." Dunleavy said.

The phone rang, and MacIntyre snatched it up. "Arson, MacIntyre." Everyone in the room tuned in as the Arson commander listened.

"Yeah...? Yeah. I see. Is there some way you can double-check?"

Dunleavy signaled to MacIntyre.

"Hang on, Chief Dunleavy wants to talk to you," and handed the receiver to him.

"Diebold? Leo Dunleavy here. No positive ID on the flashlight prints, eh? Hmm, tell you what. Compare the partials you have to the prints of a guy named Thomas Parks. That's right, P-a-r-k-s. See if you can eliminate his prints as a possible match to the ones on the flashlight. Let us know ASAP, all right, Mr. D. Very good."

Sitting on the edge of MacIntyre's desk, Dunleavy addressed the room.

"Gentlemen, if my hunch is right, the 'herky-jerky' guy the dog walker saw is better known as 'Twitch,' and is a long-time acolyte of Mr. Tutulomundo up in the Falls. That bar is, or was, run by the mob, and this Twitch character will do anything for the old man. And I mean anything—he damn near got killed in Attica guarding him one time, so disposing of a losing business property would be all in a day's work to him. Not the roughest, toughest guy in T's mob, but loyal and sneaky as hell.

"Now, if Mr. Diebold's fingerprint techs tell us that the partial fingerprints do not eliminate Mr. Parks from being the owner of that flashlight, and the dog's owner can identify Mr. Parks, we should get the 'medium size dog,' as Lt. MacIntyre called him, a lifetime supply of Alpo, Gaines Burgers, whatever he likes."

The detectives drank coffee, waiting for the results from the Identification Bureau, then ordered a couple of pizzas. Dunleavy called home to say he was working late. Another detective did the same, and his comrades laughed as the wife replied with a stream of invective that could be heard throughout the room.

"Damn, Pete, I don't think she believes you," MacIntyre said.

"Sounds like you went to the well once too often with that excuse," Asciutto said.

Dunleavy was shaking his head when the phone rang. All eyes went to the arson commander.

"Arson, MacIntyre. Yes? Yeah, yeah… yeah!"

He hung up and told the assembled policemen, "According to Mr. Diebold, although there are too few matches to make it a positive ID, the partial fingerprints on the flashlight could belong to Thomas Parks."

Cheers and whistles went up in the room. Dunleavy, seated on the edge of MacIntyre's desk with his hands clasped in front of him, waited until they quieted down. "All right. Let's get organized here. Our first priority is to draw up a warrant for Mr. Parks."

MacIntyre pointed his pen at Pete, and the detective left with a nod.

"Next, we've got to show a picture of Mr. Parks to the dog's owner and see if he can identify Twitch as the man he saw in the alley the night of the fire." MacIntyre nodded at Asciutto and he moved to get a copy of Thomas Park's picture.

"If we do get a positive identification, we can notify the Niagara Falls Police to find Mr. Parks and keep him under surveillance until the warrant's ready and we're ready to make the arrest."

"How about notifying the Feds?" the arson commander asked.

"They can watch it on the eleven o'clock news," Dunleavy said, and everyone laughed.

As the dramatic opening music for the eleven o'clock news played in the background, the TV announcer pronounced, "Buffalo police arrest suspect in arson death of Buffalo Fire Captain." The scene changed as a handcuffed Twitch was frog marched between MacIntyre and Dunleavy into police headquarters, a crowd of arson and homicide detectives following behind. The scene changed again with the announcer holding his script before him saying, "Buffalo and Niagara Falls Police tonight arrested Thomas Parks for the arson fire that killed Buffalo Fire Captain Paul Calabotta, seriously injured Firefighter Aaron Jefferson and burned several others when the closed-up Senator's Choice Tavern burned last Thursday night." Behind him, film from the fire rolled and then was replaced by formal fire department pictures of the three burned firemen in their blue uniforms and dress caps.

"Police say Parks, 53, of Niagara Falls, has been previously convicted of burglary, bookmaking and extortion, and according to police sources, is a known associate of local organized crime figures," now the background image switched again, showing mugshot photos of a much younger Twitch.

Dunleavy and MacIntyre stood out in the hallway while the sound of Asciutto's growling penetrated the walls between them and the interrogation room as the big detective stomped around the room threatening Twitch with the death sentence unless he talked. Twitch's neck and shoulders shook, but his lips remained sealed. Dunleavy looked at his watch and rapped on the reinforced glass window. Asciutto exhaled and opened the door. Dunleavy silently mouthed "five minutes" and the detective left to get himself some water. Dunleavy came inside, quietly closed the door, took a sip of coffee and walked to a bulletin board where he casually flipped through memos hanging on a clipboard there.

Gazing at a notice for a softball team sign up, Dunleavy quietly said, "Does Tutulomundo even know you lit the place off? I hear he's not there a lot of the time," he said, tapping his temple.

Twitch's shoulder jumped, but he said nothing.

"I checked the ownership of the building, Twitch. A couple of old timers, distant relatives of some friends of yours. I'm passing that information along to the insurance people, Twitch, and I'm sure they'll deny the claim when they find out." Turning around with his hands in his pockets, Dunleavy continued, "Have to hire a lawyer and sue to get the money in court from the insurance company, Twitch. This whole thing might not pay anything. Did Strazzo give the OK for this job, Twitch? *Hmmph.* Interesting. Very interesting." Dunleavy headed for the door, hesitated with his hand on the door handle, and said, "...and you've been playing with dynamite, too, haven't you? If he finds out, Squalo might be very unhappy with you, Twitch. You might think about talking to Detective Asciutto..."

Twitch's neck and shoulders trembled. He lowered his head and clenched his teeth. *I knew it,* Dunleavy thought, catching this out of the corner of his eye. *He's lined up with Strazzo.* He left the interrogation room as a recharged Asciutto barreled back in.

51.

NEW YORK STATE SUPREME COURT, PART 19, BUFFALO, 1980

Jerry Hallinan looked down at his legal pad while the assistant district attorney questioned David Scott, "the dog walker," as the papers were calling the State's eyewitness. Hallinan doodled while the A.D.A. went through the preliminary questions—the witness's name, address, employment—but took notes when he noticed the witness tense up or look away. This was Hallinan's first appearance at Twitch's trial, and he sat as second chair to the firm's founder, Geoffrey Sturges. Despite Hallinan's previous absence at this trial and casual demeanor, there had been endless hours of research and interviews done by the lawyer.

When the A.D.A. got to what David Scott, professor of art history at SUNY Buffalo, had seen on the night the Senator's Choice Inn burned, Hallinan noticed Scott taking his hands off the armrests and straightening up in his chair.

"So, Professor Scott, what time were you walking your dog the night of Wednesday, March 23, 1980?"

"I always walk him around 10:30, after I'm through with correcting papers and before I go to bed."

"And do you always walk your dog the same route?"

"Pretty much. We go through the park and down the alley

behind the buildings on Allen Street."

"Why down the alley, Mr. Scott, why not down Allen Street?"

Scott folded his hands in front of himself.

"To avoid the people bar hopping on Allen."

"I see. They disturb your dog then?"

Hallinan noticed the corners of Scott's eyes crinkle slightly.

"Sometimes, so we just go down the alley to avoid them at that hour."

"So, on the night of March 23rd, at approximately 10:30, you were in the alley behind the Senator's Choice Inn with your dog?"

"Well, yes, right where the park and the alley meet, anyway."

Eyes still lowered, Hallinan shifted from doodling to note taking, pressing down hard on the #2 pencil.

"And did you see anyone in the alley that night?"

"Yes, I did."

"Mr. Scott, please describe the person you saw behind the Senator's Choice Inn that evening."

"I saw a skinny white man, about fifty years old, wearing old clothes and sneakers. He had straight dark hair and was very nervous."

"Mr. Scott, by nervous, what do you mean?"

"He was trembling a lot. His shoulders, his neck, his arms were moving… They were moving like someone with some sort of nervous disorder."

"Mr. Scott, do you see the person you saw that night in the alley here in the courtroom?"

Scott looked over at the defendant's table where the two lawyers sat impassively. Twitch stared back at the art teacher.

"I saw him, the defendant, in the alley that night." The A.D.A. lifted his right hand from his side ever so slightly, index finger out, and taking the cue, Scott pointed at Twitch.

When the A.D.A. had finished his examination, Scott exhaled and relaxed a little.

"Your witness," the A.D.A. said. Sturges looked over at Hallinan, who shook his head. "The defense has no questions for the witness at this time," Sturges said, surprising the courtroom.

When court adjourned for the day, the firemen in the crowd worked their way out, nodding and evaluating the trial.

"They got him dead to rights," said one.

"I wish they still had the death penalty in this state," said another.

The following day, the prosecution called in their police witnesses. The policemen testifying were professional and concise. Each spoke of his expertise and experience, and Dunleavy made sure they were all well dressed and clear eyed. Most wore three-piece suits as opposed to their usual plaids and polyester. Dunleavy watched carefully as Ascuitto testified about how they discovered the eyewitness Scott. He remained straight faced and didn't growl. When he finished, Dunleavy nodded in approval. Sturges stood after Diebold from the Identification Bureau was questioned by the prosecution.

"Mr. Diebold, how many years have you been with the Buffalo Police Department?"

"As of the end of next month, thirty-two."

"How many of those years have been with the Identification Bureau?"

"It'll be twenty-six next year."

"Now, the prosecution has already established your expertise in handling fingerprints, and a very fine record it is indeed, sir. Now, as to this case, you have testified that the partial fingerprint discovered on the flashlight found in the Senator's Choice Inn after the fire cannot be ruled out as belonging to my client Mr. Parks, is that right?"

"That's correct."

"But it cannot be absolutely established as to belonging to Mr. Parks, is that right?"

"Correct."

"So how many other people in the City of Buffalo could that fingerprint belong to, Mr. Diebold?"

"There's no way of telling…"

"So, it could belong to you or me?"

"Well, individual comparisons would show if that was possible…"

"But it could belong to hundreds, thousands of people in this city, not to mention Erie County, Western New York and so forth, is that right, Mr. Diebold?"

"Yes."

"That's all, your honor."

The defense began its case the following day, and Sturges had Hallinan call the first witness, David Scott.

Hallinan waited until Scott was seated, then rose quietly, smiling slightly, fingertips just touching the table before him. In a voice just loud enough for the room to hear, he began.

"Mr. Scott, you have testified that you are a professor of art history at SUNY Buffalo, correct?"

"Yes."

"And you walk your dog, almost every night around 10:30 from your house, through Days Park and then down the alley behind the odd numbered block on Allen Street, am I right?" Hallinan came out from behind the table to just in front of it, leaned back, and rested his hands on its polished surface.

"Yes."

"Now, you have testified that you took Pollock, that's your dog's name, is it not?" Hallinan said with a smile, "to the edge of the park, and not down the alley on the night of the fire at the Senator's Choice Inn. Am I correct on that, professor?"

"Yes," Scott said, slowly dropping his chin.

"Where was this person standing that you saw that night, Professor Scott?"

"Well, behind the bar. Behind the Senator's Choice Inn."

"Do you know how far away from you he was?"

"Oh, about 40–45 feet, I'd say."

"Well to be precise, according to the Buffalo Department of Streets, from the end of the alley to the back door of the Senator's Choice Inn is fifty-three feet, Professor Scott."

Scott raised his shoulders slightly.

"Did you notice the lighting in the alley, Professor Scott?"

"There is a streetlight there at the end of the alley."

"Yes, yes there is, professor. I have here, your honor," Hallinan said, addressing the judge, "a document from the Buffalo Department of Streets that I would like to be entered into evidence. It is a plat showing the alley, the streetlights and other features of the alley under discussion."

When all parties were agreed to the exhibit, Hallinan continued. "This plat shows a sodium lamp, twenty feet above the street level, and the next light is a good seventy feet beyond it down the alley. I also have another document I would like to enter into evidence," he said, handing up some papers. "A work order from the Department of Streets dated six months ago. Both lights are due to be replaced as their luminosity is failing—but this order has yet to be carried out. This," Hallinan said, advancing towards the witness box and raising his voice slightly, "puts the back entrance to the Senator's Choice Inn halfway in-between the streetlights, the location with the least lighting and the most difficult to observe.

"Now, Professor Scott, you testified that you didn't actually enter the alley with Pollock that night. Why was that?"

"It was very cold that night. Both of us wanted to get back into the house."

"You live alone since your divorce, is that correct, Professor Scott?"

"Uhh, yes, I live alone on Days Park."

"You told no one about the person you say you saw in the alley until the police asked you about him, correct?" and Hallinan stepped within two feet of the railing between him and the witness.

"Yes, yes, that's right," Scott said, leaning back.

"What else did you observe that evening, Mr. Scott?"

"Well, about half an hour or so later, I heard the fire engines."

"Did you smell anything at the time?"

"Yes, I smelled the smoke from the fire."

"Did you go outside and watch?"

"I just went out on the front porch, it was very windy that night."

"Could you see the fire trucks from there?"

"Yes."

"Could you tell me how many there were?"

"I don't know, there were quite a few."

"So, Professor Scott, you're telling us that you could positively identify someone you only saw for a few moments in the dim lighting of an alley, but you couldn't identify the number of fire trucks on Allen Street with all their lights and sirens, is that correct?"

"I'd been in bed and half asleep by the time the firemen arrived…"

"Professor, how was the person you saw in the alley dressed the night of the fire?"

"He was wearing old clothes and sneakers…"

"Did he have a coat? It was cold and windy as you've said. What color was it?"

"I don't know, it was dark…"

"You mean the alley, or his coat? What about his sneakers? What color were they?"

"I think they were white. High top sneakers."

"Professor, what color shoes am I wearing?"

"I… I think…" and, looking at Hallinan's blue three-piece suit, said, "they're black."

Hallinan smiled and stepped back, showing Scott his brown shoes.

"My wife thought it was terrible when I left for work with mismatching clothes and shoes," Hallinan said, to mild chuckles from the gallery. Returning to a stern voice, he continued, "I've been speaking to you for five minutes now, professor, not ten feet from you, in a well-lit room, but you didn't know what color shoes I was wearing."

Hallinan shook his head and turned back to Scott, leaning on the witness box, dropping his head to Scott's level and looking him right in the eye.

"Professor Scott. You say you walk your dog, Pollock, after you get finished grading papers, correct?"

"Yes… yes, I grade papers in the evening."

"That's all I have for this witness, your honor."

Scott sprang out of the witness chair but stopped when the A.D.A. gently waved him back down so he could cross examine. He went over Scott's initial testimony and got him to repeat it, including pointing to Twitch as the man he saw in the alley the night of the fire.

Looking over at the jury, Dunleavy saw some quizzical looks and thought, *We lost some ground there.*

"The defense calls Martina Glenn," Hallinan announced, and a young woman with a blonde ponytail, dressed in blue jeans, and oxford shirt and a wide blue tie with red bison embroidered on it went to the witness box.

After she was sworn, Hallinan asked the young woman her name and profession.

"My name's Martina Glenn. I'm a bartender at Birdie's on Allen Street."

"Are you acquainted with Professor David Scott, who teaches at SUNY Buffalo?"

"Yes."

"Where do you know Professor Scott from, Ms. Glenn?"

"Birdie's. He used to come in there nights."

"And did you see him there on the night of March 23, 1980?"

"Yes."

"Did he have anything to drink that night?"

"Yes."

"What did Professor Scott have to drink, Ms. Glenn?"

"He had four glasses of red wine."

"Anything else?"

"He went down in the basement with me when I went to change a keg and we toked a joint."

"Was that a common practice of Professor Scott's?"

"A couple times a week, I'd say."

"Did Professor Scott say anything when you'd smoke marijuana, Ms. Glenn?"

"He said he needed it to 'mellow out' before he corrected papers from 'ignorant Buffalo kids who shouldn't even be in college.'"

Hallinan looked over at the jury and saw narrowing eyes and crossing arms.

"Did Professor Scott come in to Birdie's and smoke marijuana and drink after that evening?"

"Yes, a few times."

"Your honor, I object," the A.D.A. said. "What Professor Scott did after witnessing the defendant on the night of the crime is irrelevant."

"Sustained," the judge said. Hallinan thought, *Perfect. She won't have to tell the court everything the private investigator found out.*

Hallinan remembered the day his private investigator, Art Durkin, brought the bartender into his office. The secretary brought them all coffee and Art sat down next to her in front of Hallinan's desk. After Art had got her to describe Scott's visit to the bar that night, Hallinan rubbed his chin and wondered at her motivation for coming forth with this information. He looked at the detective and gave him a quizzical look. Knowing his employer, Art asked the young woman a few more questions.

"Does Scott still come into Birdie's, Miss Glenn?"

"Not since two Fridays ago."

"Why is that, Miss Glenn?"

"Because after he helped me change a keg and we smoked a joint that Friday night, he tried to make out with me."

"What did you do, Miss Glenn?"

"I shoved him away. I told him to get out of there, I had to go back to work."

"Did he do so?"

"Yeah, he left. Haven't seen the bum since."

And he didn't leave a tip I'll bet, either, Hallinan thought.

52.

NEW YORK STATE SUPREME COURT, PART 19, BUFFALO, 1980

The courtroom was filled with firemen, dressed in fire department T-shirts, talking loudly when it came time for the defense's summary. The widow and two teenaged children of Paul Calabotta were sitting directly behind the prosecutor's bench. Arson, Homicide and other policemen stood lined up behind the back row of seats. Geoffrey Sturges stood up, smoothed his tie down, approached the jury box silently, and when assured of quiet by the judge's tapping of the gavel, scanned the jury, making sure they could see his client sitting in the dock, shaking in an old dark gray suit. Sturges looked over the jury, thinking of his and his staff's analysis of them. *Middle class, a few working people. Can't speak too eloquently, or they'll think I'm a snob and I'll lose them.*

"My client, Thomas Parks, ladies and gentlemen of the jury, is not on trial here for his past actions, nor for his former, and I repeat former, associates in that life. He is on trial for a tragic fire that took the life of a gallant Buffalo fireman, a fire which also seriously injured several of his comrades," Sturges said, indicating the widow, the children and the scarred young firefighter in the gallery.

"Mr. Thomas Parks lives modestly in a house in Niagara Falls and has worked as a shipping clerk for a local trucking company for the last twelve years. On the night of the fire, he had supper at a local diner after work, went home and watched television. You have heard his neighbors testify, in this court, under oath, that they saw him enter the house around eight o'clock that evening and his car never left the driveway. They further testified they saw the glow of the television in the windows until around 10:30 that evening, and that later all the lights were out in the house.

"Against this, the prosecution and the police, in their haste to find somebody for this most heinous crime," Sturges said, thinking, *Hmm, may have gone too far with the word "heinous,"* then looking towards the gallery full of firemen and police said, "started with a name from the past, and what did they add to it? A partial fingerprint, not proven to be Mr. Parks', and a witness, a witness whose testimony must certainly be called into question in his identification of my client.

"Testimony has shown that Professor Scott has given a very vague description of the person he saw in the alley behind the Senator's Choice Inn the night of the fire, and that at a distance, in a dim light, and only for a few moments, as Scott and his dog were in a hurry to get in out of the cold. Yet Professor Scott," Sturges now raised his index finger, "who was not sober at the time, claims he can positively identify my client beyond a reasonable doubt.

"Good people, Mr. Parks, God help him, is a handicapped individual, suffering from cortical reflex myoclonus since childhood, and his condition has gotten worse with age. He is not a well man, as his doctor has testified—he is not someone who breaks into buildings and sets them on fire. And what is his motive? Certainly not money. His name is not on the insurance policy, nor is it on the deed of ownership. The people's names on those documents are not his relations or neighbors—a Mrs. Chinchonni, a widow who lives in Florida, and a Mr. Adornetto, who resides in a nursing home outside Syracuse.

"I will say now, good people, that Mr. Parks was not near that building on the night in question, had neither the physical ability nor motivation to set that fire, and the State, in a rush to judgment, has brought the flimsiest, most speculative evidence against Mr. Parks. It is impossible for me to understand how this case has gotten this far with it.

"I would ask you therefore to use your good judgment, to think carefully about the evidence, and when you do, I'm sure you'll realize that it is impossible to find Thomas Parks guilty of murder and arson beyond a reasonable doubt."

Sturges paused, then said, "I thank you members of the jury, for your time and thoughtfulness on this matter of the utmost importance, not only to Mr. Parks, but to our community. It is time to set Mr. Parks free, and to let the police find the true criminal who committed these crimes."

53.

The firemen and police stood stone-faced as the judge instructed the jury that day. The next few days the homicide detectives spent most of their time hanging around the office, waiting for the call that the jury had reached a decision. Maggiotto had asked a retired policeman to hang around the court during the day when they were deliberating, and the hotel where the jury was sequestered at night and notify him of anything he could find out. The squad jumped every time the phone rang, and finally, Dunleavy chased them out of the building.

"Dammit, there's more cases out there for you men to work on! Get out there and quit waiting around here! We've done all we can to nail this bum's hide to the wall! I'll call you on the radio when something happens!"

They all rushed to the courthouse four days later when the jurors filed into the courtroom to render their verdict.

The judge said, "The defendant will rise." Twitch and Sturges stood. Then he asked, "Ladies and gentlemen of the jury, have you reached a verdict?"

"We have, your honor," the foreman said, standing. He looked down as he said to a dead silent room, "We find the defendant,

Thomas Parks, not guilty on all counts."

The judge's dismissal of Twitch and the jury went unheard as the uproar in the gallery rose to a crescendo. Dunleavy stood like a statue and MacIntyre looked at him blinking.

"Unbelievable!"

"Who the fuck are these idiots!?"

"How the hell could they let that son-of-bitch go free?"

The denunciations got louder and more obscene as the crowd left the courtroom. Reporters crowded around Dunleavy as he followed the cohort of firemen and police out.

"Chief Dunleavy, what does this verdict mean for the murder of Captain Calabotta?"

"What will the police department do now? Do you have other suspects?"

"What justice can the family of Captain Calabotta expect?"

Over the shoulders of the reporters, Dunleavy spotted a frowning Zeke. He met his eyes and gave a brief shake of his head.

54.

BUFFALO POLICE HEADQUARTERS, 1980

Dunleavy marched silently back to police headquarters a block away from the courthouse and sat in his office with the door closed and the phone unanswered. For a half an hour, he went over all the steps they had taken to prove Twitch's guilt. Shaking his head, he finally gave it up, knowing there was nothing to be done about the verdict, no overcoming the law against double jeopardy.

Thinking of the image of the burned firefighter in the hospital and the big man sitting at his side, of Calabotta's widow and children in the courtroom, he thought, *I can't let this guy get away with it. I've got to find a way to get this bastard, no matter what it takes.* He sat there thinking, then got up and went out to the bullpen outside his office where Schoetz was sitting at his desk and Maggiotto was leaning on it.

"I tell you," Maggiotto said, jamming his index finger against the desk, "they must have gotten to one of the jurors. We had that bastard cold. What else…" He stopped at Schoetz's nodding towards Dunleavy, who was standing across the room, hands in pockets.

Turning to his superior, Maggiotto said, "Need something, Chief?"

"Yeah, Rico, c'mon in my office a minute."

Closing the door quietly behind himself, Maggiotto clasped his hands in front of himself and waited while Dunleavy paced around the room.

"Rico, we got our asses kicked today. We know it, the firemen, the newspapers, and the rest of the department know it. Hell, the whole city knows it!"

Shaking his head, the detective said, "We had that bum cold, Chief. There had to be..."

"No excuses, Rico. There's no retrying him on the same charges." There was a long silence, and then Dunleavy said in a quiet way, "I was wondering though if you and maybe some of the other guys could do something for me, when you're not too busy with other cases."

A smile spread slowly across the detective's face.

Twitch was guided out a side door of the courthouse by one of Sturges' staff and into a waiting car. They drove him to a hotel by the airport, where a suitcase was in a room for him and his red Buick was parked out back.

"Goodbye, Mr. Parks," the young lawyer said, handing him the keys in the rear parking lot, and he drove away. Twitch went into the room and immediately opened the suitcase on the bed. In it he found a small book of numbers and a quantity of cash he had asked the lawyer to find stashed above the ceiling tiles in his kitchen. With a sigh of relief, he found a number of addresses and phone numbers, including one in Trumansburg in the book. He repacked the book, grabbed the suitcase and left, driving east away from Buffalo and watching the rear-view mirror.

55.

F.B.I. SGO SQUAD OFFICE, AMHERST, 1980

Silverstein and Amodeo were getting bored listening to the wires day after day. Endless conversations of the mobsters boasting about women and where to eat took up endless hours. They told Shea they wanted to hit the street and complained about the other agents who had all the fun. Shea promised to rotate them, and finally, when they picked up a conversation Z was having on the phone in the Union Hall with a contractor about "picking up product," he turned them loose.

Bearded and long haired, Amodeo and Silverstein drove downtown. In their old Dodge Dart, they were part of the scenery. They followed Z to a construction site for the new light rail system on Main Street and pulled over. Amodeo got out the camera with the 300 mm lens.

"Where's he going?" Silverstein asked.

"Into the construction trailer. Surprised he knew where to find it, the no show bum. Huh, now he's going with some guy over to a shed. They're unlocking it…"

"That's a different place to hide dope."

"If it's dope, it's in a big enough box… holy shit, the product isn't dope, it's dynamite! This guy's putting a case of dynamite into his trunk!"

Silverstein started up the car and they followed as Z drove over to Niagara Street and pulled up in front of a clam stand. While Z ordered a dozen cherrystones, they called Shea from a phone booth.

"Wait," Shea advised. "Wait until he drives away, then pull him over in as quiet a place as possible. Park his car and bring him and the dynamite back here."

When Z finished his first dozen he took off his powder blue sports coat, tucked in a bib and ordered a second.

"Man doesn't have a care in the world, does he?" Silverstein said.

"Hell, he orders another Schmidt's with those clams, we can add drunk driving to the charges," Amodeo said. "What's that, his fourth?"

Twitch sat in his car in the parking lot on Crowley, right by the baseball field. Looking at his watch, he thought, *I know I told him to meet me by the ball park at Riverside. Maybe he thought I meant the one by the pool. Where the hell is this guy?* He started the car, was putting it in reverse then stopped. *I know I told him the ball field by Crowley, dammit.* He waited another ten minutes and started up the car again. *That slob's probably drinking in Santisero's or Andy's Lounge. I gotta get that dynamite, get the job done, square things with Strazzo.* He pulled out, wheels squealing and headed south on Niagara.

The agents pulled on their blue windbreakers and hung their badges around their necks as they watched, and when Z rolled back to his car belching into his hand they followed him down Niagara.

"There's a closed down car shop just ahead near Auburn!" Amodeo said, and Silverstein pulled out, moving parallel with Z's Cutlass Supreme. At the ramp to the shop, Silverstein hit the gas and cut Z off, forcing him into the empty lot. They jumped out, drew their weapons and got on either side of Z's car.

"FBI!" Amodeo shouted. "Put the vehicle in park and put your hands out the window where I can see them!"

"What the fuck is this?" Z shouted.

"Move now!" Amodeo said, and when Z had complied, Amodeo handcuffed him and pulled him out of the car. Silverstein jumped into the Cutlass and parked it in the back of the lot, then opened the trunk and brought the dynamite out, putting it in the Dart's. As they shoved Z into the back of their faded sedan, Twitch's Buick rolled by. Twitch continued down the street and pulled over, watching the brief commotion from his mirrors. *That's the Feds busting Z,* Twitch thought. *That's my dynamite they're snatching out of his trunk!*

In less than five minutes, the agents were driving out to the industrial park in Amherst, where Shea was waiting for them. Twitch followed them for a while, but when the traffic thinned out to almost zero in the suburbs and he was afraid of being spotted, he broke away.

Inside the industrial park, the two blue jacketed agents held the cuffed Z between them as they marched him into a room with a folding table and three government issued steel chairs. They sat him in one chair and put the contents of his pockets on the table in front of him, then stood off to either side of the door, hands folded in front of them. Shea entered, looked at Z, then began going through the items on the table.

"What the fuck is this?" Z slurred. "What the fuck do you guys want with me? Take these fuckin' cuffs off…"

"Did you read him his rights?" Shea asked, picking up a money clip jammed with bills. The agents nodded.

"I gotta piss, right now, you bastards…"

"Inventory his possessions?" Shea said, examining a Zippo lighter with "Club Zanzibar" engraved on it. Amodeo handed him the list.

"I want my lawyer…" Z sputtered.

Shea sat on the edge of the table and noticed Z's eyes were

clouding. Holding up a small vial with white powder in it, he said, "You might not want to call anyone, Mr. LaPancia. Does Mr. Strozzare know you use this stuff?"

"Where did that come from? That ain't mine."

"He's pretty old fashioned about using dope from what I hear…"

"I tell you, I gotta piss."

"And the dynamite? Where was that going?"

"I work *construshion*," he slurred. "They need it at another site."

"Hmm. Not a safe way to transport explosives, Z. Do you think your bosses would want to hear about this? Mr. Strozzare… or maybe Mr. D'Uccisore?"

Z stiffened. He thought about what Strazzo would do if he heard the Feds caught him with the coke. Or what Squalo would think about him with dynamite. His addled mind flashed to Tony R.'s arrest, and how T left him hanging in jail with no bail and he went Witness Protection several years back.

"You know, there might be a way to keep this all very quiet, just between ourselves…" Shea said.

56.

IRONDEQUOIT MOTOR INN, 1980

Twitch drove back out of town, this time staying in a motel near Rochester and watched the papers and the news for two days, but nothing about Z's arrest by the FBI came out. He called the bar on Delaware where Z liked the fresh sliced beef sandwiches and watched sports on weekends on a big screen they set up with the newest Curtis-Mathes projector for the TV. The bartender handed Z the phone.

"Yeah?" Z answered, spooning horseradish onto a Kimmelweck roll.

"Z, it's me. What happened to the package you had for me? You never showed."

"Those fuckin' guys at the job site, they been movin' shit all around… there's been inspectors from the state come by, too. We gotta be careful, you know? We gotta hold off on that piece of work for a little while, understand?"

"So you didn't get the package?"

"That's what I'm tellin' you. We gotta maintain a low profile for a while. Uncle Sam's got big eyes these days. Get it?"

"Uh, OK. I'll call you back. I been moving around some."

"Yeah, yeah, you do that," Z said, taking a gulp of beer and putting the phone down on the bar.

I've got to tell Strazzo, Twitch thought.

57.

THE WEST SIDE, BUFFALO, 1980

Z drove up Connecticut Street and pulled into the gas station, parking in the back of the lot.

"Who am I?" Amodeo quizzed him.

"Pete Carbone from Baltimore. You're the sales manager of Louis Carbone Ford in Glen Burnie out in the suburbs. Louis is your dad."

"Right," Amodeo said. "Lead the way, my friend," he said, slapping Z on the back as the mobster pulled out the keys to the social club next to the gas station. "Remember, steer the money man to me around ten. I should've lost about five Gs by then."

58.

ROCHESTER, NY, 1980

Twitch stopped in the bar in Rochester by the Kodak plant, closed the door to the phone booth and dialed the number for Strazzo. It was his third attempt, from a third location.

"C'mon, c'mon," he mumbled to himself, and he jerked when the phone was answered.

"Yes?" demanded Strazzo's whisper.

"Strazzo, it's me," Twitch said, checking to see the phone booth's wooden door was securely closed.

"I know who it is. What do you want?"

"I gotta meet with you."

"Why?"

"I'm with you, boss. I helped you—"

"Shut up, *stu gatz*. There's big ears out there."

"How about underground? I could meet you underground."

Strazzo considered the code word 'underground.' "OK," he said.

"Thanks, Strazzo. I know someone's—"

"Will you shut the hell up?" Strazzo rasped.

"OK, OK, I'll see you there. You won't regret it," Twitch said to a dead line.

59.

WILLIAMSVILLE, NY, 1980

Strazzo stood with his hands clasped behind him at the back of the church, nodding to the parishioners as they left at the end of Mass. When the church had emptied, he took the canvas bag with the collection from the wicker baskets and walked over to the rectory, putting it on the desk in the office.

"Here's the collection, Father," he said to the priest who was coming in from the sanctuary.

"Thank you, Grant. We appreciate all you've done for the parish since you moved out here, ushering and helping at the dinners," the white-haired cleric said.

Strazzo smiled and bowed his head.

"We haven't had a chance to talk, though, things have been so busy..."

"You're right Father," Strazzo said in a low tone. "I'll have to come and see you soon. I gotta run right now though, a family member is waiting for me in the parking lot," he said, pointing out the rectory window. "I must make time for family."

From the window, the priest watched him take the keys to his Cadillac out of his pocket and start talking to another man standing by a Cutlass Supreme in the lot. He thought of what he'd read and heard about him going back years. *Strozzare arrested in*

truck hijacking... Police round up suspects in union official's death...
West Side man sentenced for extortion. His suburban parishioners
mumbling about when he volunteered to be an usher. *That guy's*
mafia! How can Father let him take up the collection? He shook his
head and wondered what went on in his new parishioner's mind,
and if he could reach him at all.

"You ready for this?" Strazzo said to Z.

"You betcha," Z said. He nodded towards an old Plymouth down
the street. "They're right down there. I double checked this car, too.
There's no tracers on it, just yours."

"Good. All right, I'll see you under the viaduct."

They got into their cars and drove down into North Buffalo
by different routes. Z waited under the viaduct on Main Street
and Strazzo came up next to him a few minutes later. With the
FBI a block behind and the depressed street going under the
railroad tracks out of their line of sight, Strazzo quickly stopped
and switched cars with Z, then drove off and took the right on
Hertel before they could catch up. He drove north out of town to
Lockport and parked on Pine Street by the canal. He walked across
the bridge and looked down into the canal locks some seventy feet
below, watching the water slowly draining out of the upper lock as
a boat waited to descend into the lower one.

Strazzo walked down the hill alongside the lock to the entrance
of the stone arched cave. He hesitated just inside the entrance and
let his eyes adjust to the darkness. As he walked along the rock path
next to the water channel, what little light entered from outside
reflected green off the water onto the stone walls. He listened
carefully, but only heard the lapping of the water against the stone.
He lit a cigarette and waited, thinking about how to handle Twitch,
knowing that with T powerless, the guy had nowhere to go, no
one to depend on. Their own people were becoming undependable
when the law cornered them these days, and this guy... He felt the
.25 automatic in his belt and tapped the piano wire in his suit coat

pocket. He wondered how sound echoed in the tunnel, built 150 years ago to power the mills with the water tumbling down along the canal that once thrived above them.

Twitch was reluctant to drive back towards Buffalo and the Falls, afraid that one of Squalo's guys might spot him, but he was getting desperate and the family was all he knew. He had shown up half an hour early and checked out the location, looking for familiar people and cars, found none, then parked a block away and watched the site from the bar above the locks. When Strazzo drove by and parked, he watched for another five minutes and walked slowly down the hill to the cave.

Twitch saw the glow from the cigarette in the dark cave and approached. Strazzo stood there, eyes focused on Twitch, flicking ashes off his Chesterfield and shaking his head.

"What?" Strazzo said in a near whisper when Twitch stopped three feet in front of him.

"I helped you. I did the bomb on Squalo's house, I did the bar for you and I came back now. I was waiting for Z to get me more dynamite."

Strazzo tilted his chin up. "You failed."

"I'm on your side, Strazzo. You need me."

The underboss dropped the cigarette and crushed it under his Italian made shoe. "You screwed it up," he said. He squinted at Twitch and shook his head. "I'll get Squalo my way," he said, tapping his chest with his index finger. "My money from the fire job? The lawyer for the old people says the insurance company's still got it tied up. Says it'll take a while before they pay off, if they ever do."

Twitch shook his head and looked at the ground. "Look, Strazzo. I know one of your guys is…"

Strazzo smirked and slid a step closer, hands in his suit coat pockets. Twitch froze. Strazzo turned his head, hearing voices coming from further down the tunnel. Two teenagers were laughing.

"Let's smoke the other one," one said as they walked towards the entrance.

"Don't fall in and get the shit wet, man," the other said.

"Quit worrying, man, I got it," the first one said.

Twitch looked over Strazzo's shoulder and saw two figures silhouetted along the rock wall and heard the flick of a cigarette lighter. The smell of burning pot wafted towards them. Strazzo turned back and looked at Twitch.

"Go home and stay there, Twitch. I'll call you there when I need you." He walked past Twitch and muttered, "You never were one of us, anyway." Twitch stumbled back as Strazzo pushed past him out of the cave.

60.

NIAGARA FALLS, 1980

That night, T was awakened by what he thought was a storm. He got up, calling, "Twitch! Twitch! Where are you?"

"Don't worry, Mr. T, everything's OK," Enzo said, as debris from a nearby explosion fell on the roof.

"What? What's going on? Who are you?" The old man said. Enzo ignored him, looking out the front window at the red glow of Twitch's blazing house and picking up the phone.

"Yeah, they got his house. We're OK here," Enzo said. "And I found the old man's book."

61.

FISHKILL CORRECTIONAL FACILITY, 1980

Melvin signed up for two classes, one in accounting and another in math. It was a relief from the usual jailhouse routine, and the material wasn't hard. The math class was pretty much a repeat of his upper level high school course at Bennett, and he got an A in it. Fundamentals of Financial Accounting was also easy for him, and he figured he might be able to use that on the outside, dreaming of an office job someplace. When he took the final, he was the first one done, and the teacher nodded and smiled as he handed in the test.

"Here," the bespectacled man said, handing him a worn textbook. "This is for Fundamentals of Managerial Accounting. You're signing up, right?"

"Sure, sure."

"Excellent. I'm sure you aced this test. Read up on Managerial Accounting before the next semester starts."

"Looking forward to it. Really," and he shook the teacher's hand.

The next day, Melvin was putting a coat of varnish on the banister leading up to the Warden's office when the Captain came down the stairs looking through a sheaf of papers on a clipboard.

"Watch out, there's wet varnish on the railing," Melvin said.

The Captain stopped, looked up, checked his hand to see if this convict had already gotten him. Seeing nothing there, he stared at Melvin for a moment, then started back down the steps, and stopped again. Turning, he flipped through some papers and said, "Peters, right? I have a notice here… you're to report to the Institutional Parole Officer this afternoon at 2:00 p.m.," turned and headed back down the stairs.

Holy shit, maybe, maybe they're going to cut me loose, Melvin thought. *Next month I'll have done a year and nine months, enough for a Conditional Release.* He sat down on the steps, exhaling and looking out the big window on the landing at the grassy fields and green trees outside the prison. *Outside the walls and razor wire. Grass, not concrete under my feet. Open spaces, walking the streets again, not locked down every night.*

Melvin was escorted to the Counseling Office and sat down in front of a desk piled high with folders. The Institutional Parole Officer was a balding white man with a striped dress shirt and solid black tie with reading glasses propped on top of his head.

"Let's see here, Peters, Peters, Melvin Peters," he said as he dug up Melvin's paperwork. He put on the reading glasses. "Here we are. Now, it says next month you will have served a year and nine months, yes? With time served in the Erie County lockup, that would give you two years total and make you eligible for Conditional Release on your one to three year sentence, yes? Ummm, no disciplinary issues… and it says you helped prevent a suicide when you were in Elmira. OK. Completed two Pell Grant courses here successfully, you have a letter of recommendation from the accounting instructor and an 'attaboy' from the director of the cabinet-making shop here.

"All right, Inmate Peters," he said, putting his glasses back on top of his head and tilting back in his chair, "I see no reason why you shouldn't be granted Conditional Release on the time appointed as long as you stay out of trouble until then and agree to the twenty-five Conditions of Release listed here," he said, putting a thick sheaf of papers in front of him.

The Parole Officer began reciting the conditions of release from memory while Melvin skimmed over them in a daze.

"You will proceed directly to the area to which you will be released…

"You will reside at the following location…

"Access to your residence will be granted to Community Supervision at all times…"

Melvin signed the forms and clutched them tightly as he was escorted back to the dormitory room. *I'll read them all the way through later.* He looked at the calendar and thought, *One more month… thirty-one days and I'll be outta here!*

62.

UNIVERSITY HEIGHTS, NORTH BUFFALO, 1980

Leo came down to breakfast knotting a striped tie and sat down watching his children. Jimmy, having finished shoveling eggs into himself, jumped up with a piece of toast in his mouth, pulled on his jacket, picked up his books and headed for the door.

"Don't forget your bus pass, Jimmy," Adele said. The boy stopped, mumbled, "Right," through the toast and picked up the pink plastic I.D. card.

"Bridget's already gone?" Leo asked.

"About five minutes ago. She likes to catch an earlier bus to school," Adele said, sliding scrambled eggs from a pan onto Leo's plate.

"Perfect," Leo said, reaching for the ketchup bottle. "So, Ceelee, what rubbish is your urban history teacher spreading these days?"

Cecile smiled, knowing mention of her leftist professor aggravated her policeman father. "Hmmm, let's see. We were reading about crime going up in cities, and Mr. Roberts…"

"Oh, he doesn't call himself H.R. like he used to in his student rioting days?" Leo said, thinking of the violent protests of SUNY Buffalo's past, and the bottles and rocks bouncing off his riot helmet.

I've got him going now, she thought. "Well, he was saying that the cause of the increase in crime in Buffalo and other cities is a direct result of the increasing wealth of the capitalist class at the expense of the poor..."

"Grrrr," Leo said.

Cecile laughed and touched her father's hand, which was tightly gripping his fork.

"Well, how about your English class? Are you still reading that Russian novel? The one with the killer, uh, Raskolnikov, right?"

"Oh it's really interesting, dad. We're still discussing the 'utilitarian theory' that some people have the right to ignore the law for the betterment of society."

"What kind of people?" Leo said.

"Well, they refer to them as 'extraordinary,' people who are doing something wrong for the greater good of society."

"Yeah, but does that mean leaders, or who?" Leo said.

"Whom," Adele put in from the pantry.

"Well, they don't really say who in particular... it mostly says people who create the most good for the most people."

"Huh," Leo said, thinking.

"Jeez, look what time it is. I gotta get to school," Cecile said. She kissed her dad and mom, grabbed her books and headed out.

"You OK?" Adele asked her husband as he sat blank faced at the kitchen table, empty coffee cup in front of him.

"Huh? Yeah, I'm fine, just got a couple of things to think through," Leo said, getting up and pulling on his tan corduroy sports coat.

"You sure you're all right?"

"Uh huh," he said, kissing her and heading out to the car in the driveway. She got a brief smile from him as he closed the car door. *That Calabotta case is really getting to him,* she thought. She remembered how he had changed over the years. First, the eager rookie, walking a beat in his old neighborhood in South Buffalo. How sharp he looked in his blue uniform and the pride he took when they used him undercover with that vending racket case. Then, the bad cases—children molested, bloody car wrecks, bloated bodies found in the river. He'd stay out late with the other policemen, drinking and sharing those awful tales. Later, when the kids came along, he stopped doing that, and they had an unwritten rule never to talk about it in front of the children. He never told her much, but he did listen to the scanner, kept so low she wondered how he could hear it. The calluses on his soul usually protected him, but she could tell this case was different. He'd been beaten by defense lawyers before, and Rico Maggiotto told her after several beers at a Bills game once how "the Chief" kept a file on the ones that got away. This one with the firemen was really bugging him. When he was younger, she knew he was tempted to break rules to get the bad guys, but his conscience wouldn't let him.

He never let it affect their home life, any of it. She remembered him helping Cecile learn her catechism, and later, one time taking her aside when she was about eleven. Adele and Leo were in the kitchen drinking coffee, and they overheard Cecile talking to her friend Nancy out on the back steps.

"Did you see yesterday when Sister took Josie out of the classroom?" Cecile said.

"Yeah, what was that all about?" Nancy said.

"Had to be because she wet herself. She's done that before."

Adele stood up, and Leo, seeing she was angry said, "Wait. Let me talk to her."

Leo got up, opened the screen door and said, "Hi Nancy. Cecile, come in her a moment, I'd like to speak to you."

Once inside, Cecile looked at the ground, and Leo bent over, put his hands on her shoulders and looked his daughter in the eyes.

"Ceelee, I heard what you said to Nancy about that other girl in school. That isn't true, now is it?"

"I dunno, I heard it from…"

"You know that's gossip, don't you, Ceelee?'

"Yes."

"And remember, that's bearing false witness, isn't it?"

"I guess so."

"And even if it is true, it's nasty to say that about that girl, isn't it?"

"Yes."

"Well, what do you think you should do?"

"Tell Nancy that…"

Leo nodded, "Go on."

"That it's just something I heard…"

"And?"

"I shouldn't have said it because I don't know if it's true."

"And?"

"It's mean."

Leo nodded and stood up straight. Going out the screen door, Cecile turned to her father with an unsure look. He smiled and nodded. She went out and both parents heard Cecile say, "I shouldn't have said that about Josie. I just heard it somewhere. It's mean…"

"Girls can be so cruel sometimes," Adele said. "I'm glad you did that. I might've shouted at her. That wouldn't do any good."

"Yeah. I was just thinking about all the nasty things they used to say about a girl back in the old neighborhood on Sidway. That kid never got over it. Lived at home with her folks, never went out, never got married. Worked at a stationery store for years, keeping the books and working the counter."

Yes, Leo knew people, that's for sure. He'd gotten ahead by listening to people and learning everyone's habits in the city, in all the neighborhoods—Black, white, Irish, Polish, Italian, Indians. The one thing he always said about his job was, "They pay me to listen to all those people, dead and alive. They all eventually talk to me."

She watched him as the city changed, and saw he made a point to learn about the newcomers, Puerto Ricans, now Dominicans and Yemenis. "They're moving in up in Black Rock and way down on the West Side," he said of the Dominicans. "Even thinking of changing the school name from Assumption up in Black Rock."

After he became chief of homicide, the rate of solved murders went up, and in a couple of years, they had even cleared all of their cases. He said when one got away, "It's like Inspector Wachter would say. 'They'll screw up again, just be ready.'" His unit was the pride of the department, everyone said, but the good publicity maybe made him too sure of himself and "his men" as he called them, she thought.

63.

JERSEY STREET CAFE, THE WEST SIDE, 1980

Maggiotto drove his chief over to the West Side and parked directly in front of the Jersey Street Café, where they sat drinking coffee and reading the paper. They didn't even look up when Squalo and Enzo walked into the place just after 9:00 a.m. Walking by the detectives' car the mobsters looked at each other, but not at the lounging policemen. Inside, Squalo looked at the waiter, his hands spread wide, palms up. The waiter shrugged and shook his head as he poured their coffee.

"What the fuck?" Squalo asked.

"Dunno," the waiter said. "They been out there for an hour."

"Who!? Who is it out there?" Shea shouted, listening in to the microphones from the suburban warehouse.

"Think it might be a set up for a hit?" Amodeo said.

Shea waved him to be silent. Silverstein whispered, "Nah, they would've shot him on the street."

"We have to get cameras set up on that place!" Shea said.

Dunleavy walked into the café, the bell over the door tinkling. He took off his hat and carefully placed it on the hat rack, then turned to the two hoodlums.

"Gentlemen," he said, palm upraised. "Mind if I sit down?"

Squalo's eyes narrowed as he silently pointed to an empty chair.

Dunleavy sat, leaned back and folded his fingers in his lap. The waiter came over.

"Regular coffee, please," the policeman said, smiling. He paused, then looked at the two cousins.

"I was wondering if you fellas could help me with something?" Dunleavy asked casually.

The two nodded but said nothing.

"That's Dunleavy!" Shea said.

"Your friend Mr. Parks seems to have left town after the trial. You wouldn't know where he went, now would you?"

They looked at each other and shook their heads.

"Funny thing. Man gets found innocent, but he leaves town. Then, his house, in one of the safest neighborhoods in the Falls, blows up."

They shrugged.

"Someone might think some of his old friends were mad at him. Maybe they think he might make friends with the police… or maybe even for playing with dynamite. By the way, Mr. D'Uccisore, how are you feeling these days? Looks like all the scars are healing up. I see a little bit of hair still has to grow back on the side there," he said, brushing his fingers against his temple. "And did you manage to get a good contractor to work on your house? I know a guy I went to the academy with, does great work on the side."

"Everything's fine," Squalo replied through gritted teeth.

"Well," Dunleavy said standing up. "I won't take up any more of your time. I'm sure you've got to get to work just like the rest of us." He took a dollar out and laid it on the table along with his card. "Can't be accepting gratuities, you know." He walked to the door and opened it, putting on his hat.

"Give me a holler if you hear anything, fellas," and left, whistling.

Squalo looked at his cousin and motioned him out back behind the café. They walked down the alley, Squalo clenching and unclenching his fists.

"That bastard cop. That son-of-a bitch Irish bastard. What the hell was that all about, anyway!?"

"He's trying to get your goat, Ralph. He's pissed because Twitch got off. He wants you to think Twitch blew up your house so you'll go after him."

"That prick!" he said, stroking the skin where the hair was missing.

"We got to stay calm, Ralph. We can't be doin' the cops' job for them. We got bigger fish to fry, take care of Strazzo."

In front of the café, Dunleavy said, "Drive around the block, Rico," and when they were crossing the alley where Squalo and Enzo were talking, told him, "Stop here a minute."

They could see Squalo waving his hands around, and Enzo, palms lowered, trying to calm him down.

"Hit the horn once, Rico," Dunleavy said. The car's horn got the two cousins to look up, and Squalo to start stomping his feet. Enzo grabbed him by the shoulders and turned him away from the police car.

"I dunno what you told him, boss, but you got them fired up now, that's for sure," and both policemen laughed.

"All right, Rico. I think we got the results we wanted here. Let's head back to the office," Dunleavy said.

64.

F.B.I. SOG SQUAD OFFICE, AMHERST, NY, 1980

Dunleavy drove out to the northern suburb, to the industrial park that was fenced in and locked. The first time he had been there it took him a while to find the ribbed metal, single story building amongst ten others, thinking you couldn't get more concealed than being out here in the country like this. When he was admitted then, he still wasn't sure if he was in the right place—the agent who let him in was wearing jeans and a sweatshirt, and there were tables scattered about covered with electronics. *Looks like a TV repair shop*, he thought.

Special Agent Shea rose, scraping his chair along the concrete floor.

"Chief Dunleavy, good to see you," he said, extending his hand.

"Kevin," the older man said, looking around. *None of Mr. Hoover's gray flannel suits out here.*

"Would you like some coffee, Chief?" Shea said, walking towards the coffee machine.

"Now there's some police equipment, I recognize," Dunleavy said.

With coffee cups in hand, they walked over to where a bearded Silverstein sat with earphones on.

"We recently got the Jersey Street Café wired for sound, Chief."

"I guess most of your manpower is tied up over with the outfit on Franklin Street these days."

"Not as much as before, Chief. The boys in that locale have a lot of their non-official meetings at other locations."

And you've got an informant in that bunch you're not telling me about, either, Dunleavy thought.

"You'll be pursuing them for quite a while to come, Kevin. Have you heard anything interesting from our friend Squalo yet?"

"*Noooo,* but we did hear a prominent local police official discuss some rifts among his friends there," Shea said smiling.

Dunleavy looked right at Shea. "You have all of that conversation on tape?"

"Well, yeah," Shea said. "You never know what's going to be useful."

"I really don't think my conversation with them could be useful," Dunleavy said.

"Hmm. Do you think Twitch had something to do with the bomb at Squalo's house, Chief?"

"That's what I mean, Special Agent. I don't think that speculation could be useful to the federal attorneys."

"Maybe you're right, Chief. I think Agent Amodeo said that part was unintelligible."

Dunleavy continued, "Uh, have you picked up anything else from there?"

"Well, what we do know is that Squalo and Strazzo both expect to be T's heir apparent, and Squalo's cousin Enzo has been frequenting T's house."

"Hmmm, interesting," Dunleavy said, sipping his coffee. "So Squalo seems to have family approval for leadership. Any idea what Strazzo's been up to?"

"Nothing exciting lately. He was hanging out in Williamsville the other day, at a church of all places, Chief, and showed up back at his house out there a while later."

In other words, your boys lost him for a while, Dunleavy thought. *Headed east maybe, out towards where Twitch is hiding.*

"You probably won't get much in the café there. They've been dodging the law in and out of that place for three generations."

Shea nodded. "Any recommendations?"

"Well, if I had the resources," Dunleavy said, waving his hand about the place, "I'd sit on the two big boys, Strazzo and Squalo, and put tracers on all their cars."

Shea clenched his teeth.

"Any idea where Mr. Parks might be?" Shea asked casually.

"Disappeared bag and baggage, Agent Shea. They don't have any more use for him, he might as well have the plague. The Falls police are working on who blew up his house, but don't have any suspects yet. My guess is that it was a piece of Strazzo's work. Sooner or later he's got to reach out though, he can't go too long without a lifeline to someone, somewhere in the mob."

Which would suit you fine, you old fox. Maybe the mob might take care of what the courts wouldn't.

65.

SOUTH BUFFALO, 1980

Dunleavy got back in his car and drove back downtown towards headquarters, thinking of his next move. *Squalo was fired up, that's for sure, and sure to lash out at someone. He'd never stand for one humiliation after another, and Twitch is the target right in front of him. A little more gas on the fire and maybe when we find him, I'll slip Twitch's location to Squalo and Strazzo on the sly. That would do the trick. Twitch being out of town, in a quiet place, that would be convenient, too. If Squalo got Twitch, some close surveillance on Squalo might get him as well when he did—but he'd probably farm that job out, things were a little hot for them right now—maybe he'd put Lovejoy on the job. If this works out right, we might just roll up half the mob in Buffalo. Then the FBI with all their wiretaps, tracers and undercovers could run down Strazzo and the laborers local, and the city would be rid of those mob bastards once and for all...*

"Attention all units in the vicinity of South Park Avenue and Germania, a report of shots fired..."

Jarred from his reverie, Dunleavy turned on the lights and siren and sped down Main Street towards South Buffalo.

Gotta be right by the bar. I wonder who owns that place now?

Dunleavy stopped on South Park in front of a one-story flat roofed saloon, vinyl shingled with only a couple of small block glass windows for natural light. Looking around, he saw four patrol cars parked around the lone building in the block, uniformed policemen fanning out and a couple of trash men at the concrete garage across the street watching the scene. He pulled into the gravel lot next to the bar, where one uniform was talking to the one-eyed owner underneath a hand-painted shamrock sign advertising Balor's Pub, and another uniform was talking to a stocky man in a zip-up sweatshirt and ball cap waving his hands around in front of an unmarked large van.

"What the fuck is going on in this city!?" the man in the sweatshirt shouted as the patrolman examined a nine millimeter pistol. "I can't even do business in South Buffalo without some asshole trying to hold me up!"

Kevin Williams, the vending machine guy, Dunleavy thought.

"How the fuck am I supposed to make any money with assholes jumping me right here on South Park!? Can't you fucking cops keep these assholes under control?!"

"You say you've got a permit for this pistol, right, sir?" the young patrolman asked.

"You're goddamn right I've got a permit, otherwise you sons of bitches would lock me up instead of the criminals!"

Spotting Dunleavy, a white-shirted lieutenant who also was listening to the vendor's tirade walked over to the homicide chief. Shaking hands, the lieutenant smiled and said, "Mr. Williams is a little upset, Chief, but it doesn't look like he's hurt. Physically, anyway."

"What happened, el-tee?" Dunleavy asked.

"Mr. Williams had just finished cashing out the jukebox, pool table, cigarette machine and a couple of video games, and was putting his thirty-three dollars and seventy-five cents in his van when, according to him, 'three guys came out of nowhere' and relieved him of his cash. According to Mr. Williams, two of them carried revolvers, snatched the canvas satchel and took off on foot."

"Which direction?" Dunleavy said.

The lieutenant jutted his chin northwards and then eastwards. "I sent a couple of cars up South Park, they're going through the streets and will check out the projects on Louisiana Street if they don't spot anybody likely before that."

Dunleavy nodded towards the owner of the bar, now accompanied by a half dozen of his daytime regulars on the lot, bleary eyed in the sunlight.

"Not much information there," he said.

"Didn't know it happened," the lieutenant said.

"Fuck this place!" the vendor shouted. "I'm outta this goddamn city! I've had my vending business over twenty years, and this is it! The first time I get held up and it's in South Buffalo where all you cops come from! To hell with it! To hell with this city!"

"After the suspects got his money and ran, Mr. Williams went to his truck, retrieved his nine millimeter and fired off six shots at the ones headed east," the Lieutenant said.

"Hit anything?" Dunleavy asked.

"Not any bad guys that we can tell, and we're checking the houses on Abby and Germania, but so far, no damage down range."

"All right then, lieutenant, since there's nobody dead, I'll leave it to you, young man," Dunleavy said.

"You'll be the first one we call if anyone turns up dead, Chief," the lieutenant said, then turned back to where the vendor was still roaring at the patrolman. As Dunleavy closed the door to his car, he heard the vendor shout, "…this is what I get for the machine permit fees I pay!? You bastards asking me if I've got a gun permit!? What the fuck is wrong…"

As Dunleavy started the car, he thought about the bar and the neighborhood's history. He was riding in a patrol car, back around 1960 it must have been. *There were houses and businesses all along this section then*, he thought, noting all the empty lots now. *This joint had a working kitchen then, had a pretty good roast turkey special Thursdays if I remember. What was it called then? Ferguson's? Something Irish, that's for sure. Fogarty's. That was it. Fogarty's. Phil Maley was my partner, and there were three stick up guys working the area...*

66.

SOUTH BUFFALO, 1960

Maley looked out the patrol car window as Dunleavy drove down South Park.

"I heard that joint, Fogarty's, has pretty good food, especially the fish fry," Maley said.

"Yeah, it's not bad. Adele and I have been in there a few times," Dunleavy said.

"Leo, slow down."

"What's up?"

"There's a guy in the parking lot. Something wrong about him."

They slowed down, they turned around and cruised past the bar again.

"There he is," Maley said, indicating a man with a pock-marked face wiping his nose with his sleeve. They turned down Germania, then came back up behind the man in the parking lot.

"Hey, you! Snot nose!" Maley said, getting out of the car and gripping his nightstick. The man turned and stiffened. Up close, they saw his red-rimmed eyes and long-sleeved shirt on the hot day.

"Wha'?" the man said.

"What are you doing here?" Dunleavy demanded.

"I'm, I'm… looking for my keys. On the lot here, officer."

"Which car is yours?" Maley said.

"Uh, uh, that Ford. The red one over there," he said, sniffling.

Maley put the end of the nightstick up against the man's chest.

"Stand over against the wall there," Maley said as Dunleavy went into the bar to check. A minute later, he came back out.

"It's the cook's car," Dunleavy said. Maley spun the man around and kicked his legs apart.

"Put your hands on the wall," Maley said as Dunleavy searched him.

"You got anything going that'll stick me in your pockets, junkie?" Dunleavy said. Finding his wallet, Dunleavy looked through it.

"Edward Costello. Lives in Lackawanna," Dunleavy read.

"What are you doing up here?" Maley asked. "Casing the joint?"

"No, no, you got it wrong, man. I was drinking up here last night, lost my car, my keys," the man said.

"Bullshit," Maley said, getting out his handcuffs. "Edward Costello, you're under arrest for vagrancy and suspicious behavior."

Driving Costello to the station house, they threw questions at him.

"Where do you live Costello? You got an apartment or a house?"

"I live in an upper…"

"You gonna get sick on us? You look like you're coming down hard."

"I…"

"You get sick back there, we're going to kick your ass."

"You and your friends looking for a place to rob, skag head?"

"I told you, I was looking for my car, man."

They pulled up alongside the one-story brick station house on Louisiana Street and put Costello in a holding cell in the back of the building, where Maley quipped, "No one can hear you back here, asshole, no matter how loud you yell."

He winked at Dunleavy, and as they walked back to the desk out front said, "That should scare him. My dad says back in the old days they used their saps to get confessions that way. Too bad we can't do that anymore."

Up front, Maley and Dunleavy began filling out the paperwork while the desk lieutenant called for a wagon to transport the prisoner downtown. Two detectives, Smith and Klass, were drinking coffee there and Klass asked, "What cell?"

"Number two," Maley answered, and the two uniforms looked at each other as the detectives went back towards the cells. While the two patrolmen were still at the desk, the two detectives came out.

"You two guys. No need to call the wagon," Klass said.

"Yeah, and get rid of the paperwork, too. No need for it," Smith said, wiping his brow with a handkerchief.

Dunleavy and Maley looked at each other.

"Your vagrant has been helpful, we're going to turn him loose," Klass said. "Why don't you guys come in the reserve room, we'll explain."

Klass and Smith sat on the edge of the big wooden table while the bluesuits stood.

"That bum," Klass explained, "has admitted he's one of the three stick-up guys working the neighborhood. He and the other two skag heads are scouting out their next victim, and you guys snatched up this one."

"Good work, fellas. Damn sharp." Smith said.

"Yeah, it sure was," Klass continued. "Now, so that we catch the three of them in the act, we convinced your bum to tell his girlfriends that the best time to stick up Fogarty's bar is Sunday morning, just when they open."

"Yeah, they'll still have the money stowed in the bar from Saturday night, and almost nobody will be around," Smith said.

"Nice big parking lot, too," Klass added. "You guys are working this Sunday day shift, right?"

They both nodded.

"Excellent. Then here's how we'll work it..." and he proceeded to explain how their patrol car would be parked up Germania Street out of sight waiting, and the detectives would catch the three hold up men in a cross fire from two adjacent sides in the parking lot. They'd told their informant to hit the ground as soon as they said "police!"

"Do you think that's…" Dunleavy started to ask, but the detectives' staring shut him up.

Out in the patrol car, Leo asked Phil what he thought.

"They're junkies, right? You never know what they're going to do, right? They've been threatening people with a gun, right? They're bound to shoot somebody sooner or later. I figure we let those guys do a clean sweep and we get some of the credit, maybe even a promotion to detective out of it."

Leo came home to their flat in the First Ward after their shift. He didn't answer when Mrs. Maloney shouted "Hiya, Leo! Catch any crooks today?" when he went past her on the stairs. Adele met him at the top of the stairs.

"Everything OK at work, Leo?"

"Yeah, sure, babe. Just thinking… about the baby," he said, putting his hand on her tummy, growing with new life. "What do you think about calling her Petunia if it's a girl?"

She laughed, but in her hormonal alertness, knew something was wrong. *How does she always know when something's wrong?* he thought.

The Saturday before that shift, Leo went to church at St. Patrick's on Emslie Street. In the confessional, he recognized Fr. Lonergan's voice. He confessed to cursing, to drinking, to not paying attention during Mass, then hesitated.

The elderly priest waited, then asked, "I think there's something else, isn't there?" Leo explained the dilemma.

"That's what we're supposed to do, Father. Is it wrong?"

The Franciscan was silent for some moments. Finally, he said, "These are bad men, but you will be worse than they are if you go along with their murder."

Leo couldn't say anything. He blessed himself and rushed out of the confessional and the church. Awake that night, he thought, *What am I going to do? Should I try to talk to the detectives, tell them it was wrong? They'll think I'm a sissy. Word will get around. Should I tell Phil we can't do this? Just stay patrolling around the streets, let them ambush those junkies and stay out of it? That priest would say, doing nothing is the same as taking part in it.*

Maybe I should talk to the Lieutenant. But he's been after us to catch these guys, talks about it at every roll call. He never says anything when a suspect gets roughed up.

When Sunday came and Leo walked into the station house, the detectives were shaking hands all around with the off-going night shift at roll call.

"What happened?" Maley asked.

"They got the stick up guys working the neighborhood," one guy said. "They tried to hold up the liquor store over on Vandalia last night."

"Yeah, man," said a rookie patrolman. "And the owner turned a shotgun on them!"

"What happened to the robbers?" Dunleavy asked.

"All three in the hospital. Two got blasted in the store, one got his ass full of buckshot on the way out," Klass said. "Now there's gotta be a trial and all that bullshit for those lowlifes," he said, looking right at Leo and Maley.

Driving back to headquarters from Balor's, Dunleavy thought back to his feelings back then, when the ambush didn't happen. *It felt like a thousand-pound weight came off my shoulders. I remember exhaling and not saying anything the entire shift to Phil or anybody else.*

Now I'm trying to set up a lowlife myself.

He's the killer, I'm sure of it.

His own will do it, not us.

I can't let him get away with killing that fireman. And those other two boys. Those burns.

It's your pride. They beat you in court and you can't stand looking like a fool on TV.

It's murder. Any way you look at it, it's murder.

67.

F.B.I. SGO SQUAD OFFICE, AMHERST, NY, 1980

Shea, dressed in a gray suit and black raincoat carried in a case of Genesee beer and Silverstein toted several boxes of Bocce pizza while the rest of the squad sat at the warehouse table waiting for them.

"It's on, men!" Shea said. "The Federal Attorney is drawing up the indictments now and the Agent in Charge thinks this is the best operation he's seen. Now, let's turn on the recordings and celebrate Buffalo style!"

They all cheered, then quieted down to grab slices of pizza while they listened to the tapes from the social club.

"He's gotta be good for it," Z could be heard saying. "They've got two car dealerships in Baltimore."

"He paid back the first five and the vig on time, yeah, I guess he's good for it," Enzo said.

Another cheer went up as the agents twisted open their beers.

"That's what I want to hear, men, a bona fide conspiracy!" Shea said. "Loansharking on tape! And since these guys all have recent records, violations of the RICO statutes. An outstanding job, men, just outstanding. And to you, *Mr. Carbone,* he said raising his beer bottle, I say *salute!*"

They all raised their cans to Amodeo and said, "Salute!"

68.

TRUMANSBURG, NY, 1980

"I found him, Chief," Maggiotto said from a pay phone in Trumansburg.

"Outstanding, Rico. Where is he?" Dunleavy said, making sure his office door was closed.

"Holed up in a motel out here by Lake Cayuga. The State Troopers spotted his red Buick."

"Did they tell anyone? Make any reports?"

"No sir, I asked them to keep this *sotto voce*."

"Excellent work, Sergeant. What's he been up to?"

"Drove out to this house outside the little downtown they got here in Trumansburg. Goes up this road in the woods and heads down a long driveway. I had to park the car and follow him on foot so he wouldn't spot me. Remembered to bring binoculars, too. Twitch walks up to the house, and when he's at the front door, this guy comes out from around the side of the house in his bathrobe and our boy jumps sideways. Twitch talks to the guy for a few minutes, the guy points a couple times down the driveway and Twitch turns around and leaves. Not a friendly type, I guess. The guy at the house watches him until he drives away, then comes out, looks around the property. Looks like he had a weapon stashed under his robe, maybe a shotgun from what I could see."

"Did you get a look at the guy in the house? Recognize him?"

"White male, around fifty years old, blonde hair turned mostly gray. He keeps looking around when Twitch shows up, doesn't let him get close, gives him the bum's rush. It doesn't look like our boy is too welcome. I don't know this guy, but I'd recognize him again. Also got this new guy's address."

"Great, Rico. I want you to check one more thing at the County Courthouse in Ithaca, then c'mon back, and let's figure out who this mysterious friend of Twitch's is."

69.

DOWNTOWN BUFFALO, 1980

It wasn't the first time, Adele thought. *Hell, he's been doing this since he was walking a beat down in the old neighborhood,* and shook her head when Leo told her he had to head down to the county building for a couple of hours. He'd taken off that weekday morning and they'd planned on doing some gardening.

"The tomatoes are getting taller," she said. "We've got to put the bigger stakes up so they can keep growing upwards. They're almost ready to pick."

"I know, I know, dear. This shouldn't take long. I just have to look up some records this morning, and I'll be back. I'll pick up some more chicken wire over at George's hardware on my way back, too. We'll need that or the squirrels will get them."

"Your hat, Leo."

"Huh?"

"Your hat. You almost forgot your hat," she said, handing him the fedora. "Can't have the Chief of Homicide out in public bare-headed," and smiled as he adjusted it with a slight tilt to the right, the way he did when they were young. She kissed him and watched him go out the back door. He waved as he got in the car, and she waved back, thinking, *He hasn't been like this since... I dunno when.*

At police headquarters, Dunleavy took the name Maggiotto had found listed for the house in Trumansburg to the Identification Bureau. They searched for the name Andrew Rakestraw in the department's criminal records but found no yellow sheet, no intelligence reports, nothing. *No record at all. Rico couldn't find his picture anywhere in the mugshot books, either. How is a guy with no record associated with Twitch, then? He hasn't lived in that house by Lake Cayuga all his life. Rico says the land records in the Ithaca Courthouse listed him as living at the Hotel Huron here in Buffalo when he bought the place. Where did he come from before that?*

In the basement of the Erie County Building, Dunleavy went to the County Clerk's office where they kept the records of all the real estate transactions in the county and looked up the name Rakestraw in the Grantees Index. The clerk flipped through the alphabetical files and found his name and the dates of two sales, one in 1961, one in 1972.

"You have to look these transactions up in the libers—that's the books, over there," she said, pointing to a room with racks of six-inch thick ledgers. "Check for the dates on the books and it'll give you the transactions you want."

Dunleavy went into the room and looked around. It was low ceilinged with exposed ductwork and small dirty windows fronted by rebar facing the street. Several people had pulled out ledgers and hauled them onto the slanted metal desks where they were copying information about real estate transactions. Dunleavy walked along the shelves, checking the dates on the ledgers until he came to one he wanted. He rolled the heavy bound book off the shelf and put it on an open desk. He flipped through the musty smelling pages until he found the name Rakestraw, Andrew. One property listed to him was the shop with the apartment above on Ashland. Then he found another property listed to Andrew Rakestraw. *Moreland Street. Bingo! Right in the middle of Lovejoy! I've got you now, you son of a bitch!*

He carefully wrote down the addresses and started whistling to himself. As he left the land records room, the clerk asked him if he needed any help.

"Uh, no, no thank you. I was just thinking I've got to get to the hardware store… and stop by and see an old friend for a beer," he said, rubbing his chin.

70.

THE WEST SIDE, 1980

The next day, with the tomato plants staked and secured with chicken wire, Dunleavy left headquarters early and headed up the West Side to a corner tavern with big picture windows in its green painted front and white semi-circle concrete steps leading inside. Closing the door quietly, he stood looking the length of the polished mahogany bar until he caught the bartender's eye. The bartender, a short man with slicked down black hair and a lined face, stiffened at the sight of Dunleavy and tilted his head ever so slightly sideways towards the policeman. The man at the bar he'd been talking to looked over and shut up. Dunleavy walked to an open spot at the bar and remained standing there, fingertips resting lightly on the beveled edge as the barman approached slowly.

"Tom, it's been a while," Dunleavy said.

"It has, Lieutenant. It has," the bartender said, leaning forward and wiping down a spot in front of Dunleavy.

"Well, the baseball playoffs will be starting soon, Tom, and the Bills' and Sabres' regular seasons start up as well," Dunleavy said quietly, casually looking over the shelves behind the bar. "The way Brett, Wilson and MacRae are hitting for the Royals right now, I don't think the Yankees can take them."

Turning to the other customer at the bar, Dunleavy said, "Who are you betting on, my man?"

The man shook his head. "Nobody. I don't follow it, couldn't tell you."

Glancing back at the papers and envelopes slotted between the bottles, Dunleavy said, "I'm hoping there's nothing back there, Tom. I'd hate to have to wreck your day business with a search behind the bar just now."

"No, no, Lieutenant, everything's completely kosher here. I wouldn't do anything to get Buddy's license suspended or anything like that."

"Well, I'm glad to hear that, Tom," Dunleavy said, sitting down and dropping his hat on the bar. "You know, I think I'll have a Labatt's 50 there," he said, pointing at the taps, "and a little information about your neighbors across the street," he said, indicating the small shops across the street on Ashland.

"Sure, sure, what do you want to know?" Tom said, pouring the Canadian ale.

"Who runs the antique shop over there, the one called 'The Antique Depot?' It's got a big oak dresser in the front window."

"Uh, a guy named… Andy. Drinks B.V. and water, likes our shrimp cocktail. Stays upstairs of the shop when he's around."

"What else?"

The bartender shrugged as he set the beer glass in front of the policeman. "Not much. He's not there much. Even less than the weekend warriors who run the other antique shops over there."

"What's he look like?" Dunleavy asked, taking a large sip of the lager.

"Mmm, average height, not fat, blonde hair turning gray, maybe fifty years old."

"Ever see him with anyone?"

Tom shook his head. "Nope, always by himself. Some guys move furniture in and out every once in a while."

Finishing his beer, Dunleavy stood up and put his hat on. "How much do I owe you, Tom?"

"That's on us, Lieutenant," Tom said, rapping his knuckles on the bar.

"Now, Tom, no decent bartender gives the first beer free to a customer," Dunleavy said, leaving a dollar and his business card on the bar. "Give me a call next time you see him, all right? The wife is looking for a nice dresser."

"OK," Tom said, picking up the card and the dollar bill with a sigh of relief as Dunleavy walked out of the bar.

71.

ITHACA, NY, 1980

Twitch checked that the curtains in his room in Ithaca were closed tight and counted the cash he had left in the suitcase. It was down, way down. He jumped when he heard a bunch of people out in the hallway. *Must be parents' weekend at the college, the damn motel is full.* He opened up the address book and looked through it again, noting all the check marks next to the names. Nobody left he hadn't tried to connect with, Utica, Kingston, even Canada. Some blew him off, some hung up on him, some never answered. He shivered when he thought of how Lovejoy snuck up on him when he went to his house. *I kept quiet about him all these years and he wouldn't even talk to me.* He'd have to try the ones who didn't answer again.

If only I could get through to T, he thought. *He could make some calls and get me set up someplace else. What I know about Z, I could use that and I'd be back in somewhere.*

72.

FISHKILL CORRECTIONAL FACILITY, 1980

One year, nine months inside, Melvin thought on the day they were kicking him loose. The paperwork said he was released three months early for time served in the County lockup before he'd gotten sentenced, but the guards said it was because of overcrowding. They gave him a pair of khakis and a white shirt with a collar, and one guard led him to the front gate where the guard with the rifle in the tower looked down and watched him silently. His escort called to open the gate, and as Melvin passed through, said, "Don't come back."

Melvin looked around. Beyond that twelve feet of fence and razor wire he was finally off Planet Prison. He was in an entirely different world, one that smelled like cut grass, not the strong disinfectant smell from the green soap balls and bleach they used to wash the floors. Cars were driving by on the highway outside the gate. He wanted to dash across the road and over to the wide green lawn there and run, run, run, never looking back until clanging cell doors, disembodied yells, narrow tiers and shiv carrying inmates were utterly out of his head. A black van marked New York State Corrections idled near the gate and a blonde corrections officer about his own age wearing aviator sunglasses leaned against it.

"C'mon, Peters," the C.O. said, "Time to get gone from here."

Melvin opened the passenger door to the van cautiously. *What's the rules on this?* he thought. *I'm out. There are no rules about opening car doors on this side of the wire.*

"All right!" Melvin said, and got in the van. The C.O. handed him a bus ticket and a voucher for five dollars.

"That's your ticket back to Buffalo, and a voucher for food. There's a place called 'Newburgh Lunch' right across from the bus station if you've got time before the bus pulls out, or you can use it when the bus stops along the way."

The C.O. chewed gum and listened to Ozzy Osbourne's 'Crazy Train' on the van's radio on the way to the bus station, another detail in a day's work. For Melvin, excitement built with every yard they were away from the razor wire and the incessant howling of prison. He silently took in every green space, every tree, every sign pointing to somewhere else along the rolling hills of the countryside. As the van rumbled over the dark steel bridge across the Hudson, he watched the sparks from welders' torches fall into the river as a second span under construction advanced. He stared down at the choppy brown water and watched a blue and white tugboat pull a barge far below and wondered where they were going, what were they towing.

His imagination came back to the van when they pulled into downtown Newburgh and slid into the angled parking spot in front of a small gray block building. Melvin sat there for several seconds, unsure of what to do.

"Hey man, this is where you catch the bus," the C.O. said. Melvin shook his head, tucked his bag under his arm, and as he got out, the C.O. repeated the message he'd gotten at the gate.

"Don't come back."

As the van pulled away, Melvin stood in front of the station doors, unsure of what to do.

"Excuse me," an elderly couple said, maneuvering their suitcases around him.

"Oh, yeah, sorry," Melvin said, and walked into the station. He hesitated again, then walked up to the counter and put the bus ticket in front of the clerk who didn't look up.

"The 9:10's on time," the clerk said, glancing at the ticket. "It'll pull out front in about fifteen minutes."

Melvin looked at the four buses parked diagonally in the lot.

"Which one is mine?" he asked.

"The one marked 'Buffalo,'" the clerk said, shaking his head. "It'll be the last stop."

Melvin had more questions—*What route does it take? What towns does it go through? Does it go along the river? Are there mountains along the way?* But the clerk said "Next," and Melvin got out of the way as a large family, all of them speaking rapid Spanish, stepped up. The father kept repeating "Port Authority? Port Authority?" to the clerk as he bought tickets for their ride south to New York.

Melvin looked around the waiting room and sat on one of the steel folding chairs scattered around. The elderly couple who'd brushed past him at the entrance looked him over and edged away. When the Latino family walked away from the counter, the dad looked at Melvin and steered his wife and children to the other side of the waiting room.

They all know I just got out, Melvin thought. On the bus the passengers settled into groups. The older folks sat up front near the driver, the college kids went in the back to party and the business people went to sleep in the middle seats as soon as they had parked their bags overhead. Nobody sat next to Melvin the entire trip, but it didn't matter. He stared at the river, at the mountains covered with green trees and wispy clouds, at the small towns with cast iron fronted buildings on dying Main Streets. Flute columned commercial buildings now run by Catholic Charities. County Social Service agencies in shut down department stores. Dollar Stores and Save-A-Lots in strip malls at the edge of town.

He watched the people get off and on, wondering, *Who lives in these little towns? What do they do there?*

When he got back to Buffalo, Aunt Erica and Uncle Bernie were waiting for him at the cement and steel Art Deco station. They both smiled when they saw him come into the waiting room carrying a laundry bag and dressed in the stiff prison issued clothes, and Aunt Erica hugged him and kissed him. *Perfume,* he thought, *I haven't smelled that in two years.* Uncle Bernie shook his hand and said, "Welcome home, Melvin." When they walked out onto Main Street to catch the city bus, Melvin thought, *Everyone who sees me knows I'm a convict—but Uncle Bernie and Aunt Erica don't care,* and he put his arm around the fragile old lady that was taking him in again. When they got on the bus, Bernie put the money into the fare box for him and Erica said she had a roast cooking for him in the oven. She poked his ribs and said, "You lost weight, boy," and stared with concern.

When they got to the projects, Melvin could see nothing had changed there and his shoulders tightened up like they had in the yard. Kids hanging along the edges of the buildings, waiting for some action. Trash scattered across the lobby floor in the building. The battered elevator doors not closing properly. The stench of urine and spilled wine in the hallway. Once inside the apartment, he relaxed again when he smelled the roast cooking and saw the knick-knacks and doilies on the polished wooden end tables. Aunt Erica's plants growing on the windowsills. When Erica went to hang up his jacket in the closet, Melvin saw Bernie's fishing pole there. *Wow, going down to the river and throwing out a line. Just watching the water go by,* Melvin thought.

"Been fishing much, Uncle Bernie?" Melvin asked.

"Never go anymore. Too much trouble out there," Bernie said, pointing outside at the open spaces between the projects' buildings where the gangs hovered.

After they ate, Bernie went to his easy chair and turned on the TV.

"What do you want to watch, Melvin?" Bernie said and Melvin thought, *and there won't be any fights over what channel to watch either.* "Let's see, we've got *Benson*, *WKRP in Cincinnati* and *Quincy*. What do think?"

Loni Anderson's big boobs, Melvin thought, another urge stifled for nearly two years coming alive. "How about *WKRP*, Unc?"

They stayed up late watching TV that night, *No bed check!* and when Melvin went to his room, he put the fabric softened pillow up against his nose and smelled it for a good ten seconds. When he turned out the lights, he gazed out the window at the humming lights that illuminated the high rise buildings of the project and thought, *What the fuck do I do now? I got to get out of these projects once and for all before this place drags me down again.*

73.

BUFFALO POLICE HEADQUARTERS, 1980

The clerk came into his office carrying a mail bag with the most recent flyers from the Department of Parole listing convicts about to be paroled and put them on Dunleavy's desk. The flyers had front and profile pictures of the parolees and the name and phone number of the individual's parole officer. These flyers were issued to the municipalities where the criminals lived and where they had been most active. Dunleavy always looked them all over carefully, then had copies made for his unit before sending them down to the Detective Bureau. He nodded to the clerk and examined the flyers. This time there were three names that caught his eye.

Dominic Doyle, burglarizes commercial locations. Likes to go in through the roof. We just locked his cousin and brother up, but now that he's out, nobody's business in South Buffalo is safe.

Randy Emerson. Promising boxer, junkie. I wonder if he got off the heroin in there.

Melvin Peters. Conditional Release. The college boy got involved with the Pythons. The image of his mother's bloodied corpse on the liquor store floor came to mind. He looked for the name of the parole officer assigned to Melvin, picked up the phone and dialed his number over in Community Supervision.

"Parole and Supervision, Herman here."

"Brian, Leo Dunleavy here. How's tricks?"

"You know, they come, they go. Why? One of my good behaviors not behaving?"

"No, no, nothing like that, Brian. There's a guy, just got out of Fishkill on Conditional Release, named Melvin Peters who's being assigned to you. I was wondering if you could let me know from time to time how he's doing?"

Herman smiled, knowing Dunleavy. "Another potential murderer, Leo?"

"No, I don't think so. Hopefully he's just the opposite. He got caught up with the Pythons but I don't think he's in too deep yet."

"Hmmm, according to my report here... he was initially sent to Elmira. Helped save another inmate from suicide, hmm, that's different. No discipline problems... was transferred to Fishkill, got a Pell Grant, passed two courses, one in math, another in accounting... also worked in the cabinet shop. Got out on Conditional Release... uh, yesterday. Well, I'll be seeing Mr. Peters here shortly then and will give you a call and pass on my impressions of him. Why the interest, Leo?"

"Just a hunch. Didn't strike me as having any criminal ambitions, wasn't a smart ass, was actually going to college for a little while. Did you say he was working in cabinetmaking shop there?"

"Yeah, fixing desks, making furniture, stuff like that. All right, I'll get him set up, let you know what's up."

"Thanks, Brian. Oh, by the way, I've got tickets for Jimmy McGuire's retirement party..."

74.

DOWNTOWN BUFFALO, 1980

Riding the bus downtown, Melvin looked at the paperwork he'd signed at the Parole Officer's before he'd left prison. *Conditions of Release* it read at the top. There were twenty-five of them, including the one that said he was required to report to the Community Supervisor's Office at 238 Main Street, Buffalo, within twenty-four hours of his release. The bus took him past the Main Place Mall and he got out in front of a small dark gray colored building that looked like it had been a bank. It had a metal dome that was bronze colored and corroding, and there were busted windows throughout. *This can't be it,* he thought. There was a lighter colored L-shaped high rise on two sides of the old bank building and Buffalo Chamber of Commerce was engraved on the lintel above the front door of the high rise. The windows on the building hadn't been washed in months, but he noticed the number 238 etched into the glass transom window above the brass revolving doors. *This must be the place,* he thought, *in the land that time forgot.* He looked at the directory in the lobby with the cracked tile floor and found the Division of Parole Office listed on the tenth floor. Getting on the elevator, he thought he caught a whiff of grass as the car creaked up the building. On the tenth floor, he saw a door marked New York State Division of Parole on an old fashioned frosted glass window in an oak framed door. He looked at the clock when he entered the outer office. *9:05. Good. I'm early.* Going up to the counter, he cleared his throat and quietly said to the woman there, "I'm here to see someone in Community Supervision."

Not looking up, she handed him a clipboard and said, "Sign in here please. Is this your first time in the office?"

"Uh, yes." Dropping his voice even lower, he said, "I was released yesterday."

Not one of the ten or so other men seated on the folding chairs behind him in the office looked up. *I guess they're all ex-cons like me.*

"All right, Mr... Peters," she said, looking at a file. "Have a seat and Mr. Herman will see you when he's finished with the other parolee."

Melvin sat down, and parolees came and went. He saw the dark paneled wooden door with Herman's name on it, and a white man with short gray hair in a shirt and loose tie came out, shaking his head.

"Kathy, call Deputy Wilson in here, please."

The office manager got on the phone, and a gray uniformed sheriff's deputy quickly appeared. Herman signaled him into his office, and moments later the deputy was leading an emaciated man over forty with a shaggy Afro out of the room.

"Wha'? Wha'd I do?" he mumbled as he staggered out. A few minutes after he was gone, the office manager's phone buzzed and she said, "OK," hung up and looked at Melvin.

"Mr. Herman will see you now."

Melvin straightened his tie and walked into the parole officer's office, the desk and all the chairs but one stacked with files and papers.

"*Siddown...* Mr. Peters," Herman said, looking at his open file. He read for a few moments, then muttered, "Oh yeah, the Chief's boy..."

Melvin tilted his head and knitted his brows.

"OK, Mr. Peters," he said, pointing at the door. "You saw my previous client leave? In the company of Deputy Sheriff Wilson?"

"Yes sir."

"Don't be like him. He's been violated. Heading back to Attica. Reeking of dope and so stoned out of his brain he passed out on me. No need to continue the interview. No need to waste time sending in his urine test."

Herman flipped through Melvin's file, then put his elbows on the desk, folded his hands and leaned forward, looking Melvin in the face.

"All right. This is your first time here. You live at your aunt and uncles.' Be there every night by ten o'clock. The first thing you do is go out and start looking for work. While you're looking for a job, you are required to put in three applications a week, minimum. That's two special conditions I'm adding to the twenty-five you already signed off on. When you find a job, notify this office immediately. You need to bring verification of employment, like a pay stub, to me, here. If you lose your job, inform this office immediately. No drug use, ever. There's a urine test every time you come in. You come here, on time, every week at the appointed time that Kathy, the office manager, outside there, gives you. If you comply with all the conditions, I may adjust that to twice a month after half a year. Any failure to carry out these required tasks and you can be violated. You know what that means?" He pointed with his thumb behind him. "*Pfft*. Done. Back to serve the rest of your sentence. Do you understand all that?"

"Yes sir."

"All right. You were in Elmira, helped prevent a suicide there, it says." Herman looked at him sideways and paused. "Ahh, it doesn't matter, it got you up to Fishkill and you didn't fuck up, even got Pell Grants and took courses. Passed them, too. If you decide to continue your education, notify me and we'll see about adjusting your curfew as needed. I recommend Erie Community.

I know people there and it's close by. Cheap, as college goes, too. Any questions?"

"If I do everything else, can I find my own place to live?"

"Stay at your aunt and uncle's until the end of sentence and you get released from community supervision. Save your money, stay out of trouble. Don't forget, you are not to associate with any known criminals. None. Under any circumstances. You see them, walk away, I don't care if it's in McDonald's, in the park, wherever. Got that?"

"Yes sir."

"All right, Melvin," he said standing up and reaching out his hand. "Don't screw this up and wind up like that last guy who was in here. Keep your nose clean for a year and you'll be able to go where you want."

Melvin stood and shook his hand.

Herman sat down, closed his file and put it in the large heap to his right. As Melvin went out, he buzzed the office manager and took another file from his left. *He might make it,* he thought. *He just might. Even Dunleavy thinks he's got a chance,* and he cleared some papers out of the way to access his Rolodex and find Dunleavy's number.

75.

THE EAST SIDE, 1980

Melvin sat at a table in the corner of the Carrol's Hamburgers on Broadway drinking Pepsi and looking at the *Courier Express* want ads. *Just three pages worth,* he thought. *This fucking city, it's only gotten worse since I went in.* He saw a few bookkeeper's jobs, but figured they would go to women, *and sure as hell not to an ex-con like me* and skipped over them. He loosened the tie he had borrowed from Uncle Bernie and was circling a carpenter's job when the door to the place crashed open and two guys came rolling in laughing, trying to close the door on the third. Melvin looked up and spotted Roland, Itchie, and Kelvin jostling each other as they approached the counter. The lady behind the counter looked at them. Melvin stiffened, thinking *Pythons* and remembering the parole officer's warning about associating with known criminals.

"What are you boys up to?" the woman behind the counter said, hands on hips.

"Nothin', Miz Roberts," Itchie said. "Just getting some pop."

Roland looked over and spotted Melvin.

"Hey, man, look who it is," Roland said, gazing red-eyed over at Melvin. *High,* Melvin thought.

"Hey, hey, he's out," Kelvin said, and the three of them came over to Melvin's table. They started exchanging daps. Melvin didn't know the latest ones in the neighborhood, but kept his hands moving with theirs.

"Yeah, man," Roland said, pointing at Melvin with a cocked finger. "You're looking sharp, brother." The others nodded in agreement. "Got the want ads and everything. Goin' straight, good man." Then in a lower voice, "You back over in the Towers at Uncle Bernie's?"

Melvin nodded and quietly said, "Uh huh," as Mrs. Roberts looked at them through narrowed eyes.

"Same phone number?" Roland said.

"Yeah, same, same," Melvin said as Itchie ordered their drinks.

"Shit, we'll have to get together, brother quiet man," then leaning forward, added, "you kept your mouth shut about Kisha, and Bowie said you didn't give nothing up about them either."

Shaking his head, Kelvin said, "Terrance and Bowie going to be gone for a long time, but said you were righteous, brother."

They picked up their paper cups and saluted Melvin with them as they walked out. Mrs. Roberts looked at them, then at Melvin and shook her head.

76.

THE EAST SIDE, 1980

Aunt Erica noticed Melvin was jumpy every time the phone rang.

"Might be a job offer," Melvin said.

She smiled. "It will take time, Melvin, but the good Lord is watching over you."

Melvin picked up the phone and answered, looking to see if she'd gone into the kitchen. "Hello?"

"Melvin, my man!" said Roland.

"Hey, Roland, what's up?"

"Hey, there's a party tonight over at Kelvin's. You absolutely, positively have to be there."

"Uhh, I dunno, Roland. I gotta be careful, you know?"

"Don't worry about that shit, brother. Just a few of the people from the neighborhood will be there. Kelvin's got a place in a house now, away from the projects."

"Oh yeah, where?"

"Over on Archie Street. It's his dad's place now."

"Well…"

"Look, just stop by early, have a beer, say hi. You can even drink pop if you got to."

Melvin thought about it. *These guys don't get wound up until after midnight, it should be OK…*

"Kisha said she'll be there early, too. She's gotta be at work early at the office job she's got."

Melvin thought about Kisha in jeans that looked like she'd had to jump off a rooftop to get into them.

"I might make it, but it's gotta be early. Curfew from the Parole, you know?"

"Yeah, sure, Melvin, stop by early, it's number 138, in the upper. Come in by the side door."

Roland did time for stealing cars. Shit, most of those guys have been inside. Maybe I should skip it. Nah, it's at Kelvin's dad's house, it'll be OK.

77.

THE EAST SIDE, 1980

Melvin looked at the house on Archie from across the street. The sun had just gone down, and he gave himself until 9:00 p.m. to hang out. *Just like some little kid,* he thought. The lights were on upstairs, and he could see three or four people moving around up there, and at least one was a girl. *Was that Kisha?*

The people downstairs didn't seem to be home, and he could barely hear the music as he crossed the street. The side door was open, but he banged on the screen door anyway.

"C'mon up!" he heard Kelvin shout from upstairs. He went in, and when he made the turn on the stairs, saw Kelvin and another guy he didn't know smiling down at him.

"Hey, Melvin!" Kelvin greeted and the other guy smiled, Miller High Life in hand. Roland came to the top of the steps and handed him a beer.

"My man, back from the joint!" he said, clinking bottles. *Oh shit, it's starting already, maybe I shouldn't have...*

"Hiya, Melvin," Kisha said, coming towards him, arms out for a hug. Her hair was short and straightened, and yeah, she had jeans on. "Oh, we missed you," she said, kissing him. She took him by the hand and led him to the couch in the living room.

"You lost weight, Melvin," she said, smiling and jabbing him in the ribs.

"Yeah, a little, been working out, you know."

She looked him up and down, put her hand on the back of the couch and slid a little closer to him.

Later, Melvin got up to use the bathroom. *That second beer went right through me.* When he came out, the clock in the kitchen read 9:30 and he noticed the place was filling up. *Shit, I gotta go.* He looked in at Kisha and was thinking of what to say when he heard the crash outside. Everyone went to the front windows and looked. There was an old Chevy out there that had just rear ended a polished Chrysler.

"Oh shit, that fool just hit Big Snake's ride!" Roland said. They all started downstairs and Melvin heard the Chrysler's heavy door slam and someone shouting, "You dumb, no drivin' motherfucker!"

As they made the driveway, the other driver shouted back, "You don't own the street, motherfucker! Get your hooptie outta da way!"

Melvin looked at Kisha. "I gotta get outta here, baby, right now."

"I know, I know," she said, as he looked for the best way around the argument that had erupted between the Python's president and the guy with the Chevy. Melvin heard, "Fuck you, you bitch!" and then the *kapow, kapow, kapow* of automatic pistol fire.

"Get inside, Kisha!" he shouted as the people in the driveway headed for safety. Melvin looked, and she nodded as she headed inside. He ran through the backyard, over the fence and kept on going as fast as he could run. He was still a few blocks from home when he heard the sirens coming as he hit Broadway. He got to Sycamore when the police car, squealing wheels, came up around the corner from Elm and bounced over the curb in front of him. The two blue shirted patrolmen got him on the ground and were handcuffing him when he shouted, "I didn't do nothing! I was headed home!"

"Then why were you running, my man?" the Black cop said,

showing him the sweat he'd wiped off Melvin's forehead.

"Car 4-West to radio," the white cop said into his microphone. "We've got a runner here over on Sycamore," and tossing the microphone back into the car, helped his partner pull Melvin up by the arms and stuff him into the back seat of the police car.

Dunleavy listened to the call on the scanner and thought, *Steck's the squad leader tonight, he should be able to handle it,* but kept listening as the patrol cars and detectives called in their responses. When the suspects and witnesses were all in custody and the victim was confirmed dead he called downtown and spoke to Homicide's on duty supervisor.

"What do you have Danny?"

"Shooting on the street, outside a house party. Looks like some dork slammed into Big Snake's vehicle, gave him some mouth and got shot for it. We've got the Snake in custody and we're working on six potential witnesses."

"All right, you've got everything under control?"

"Yessir. We'll probably still be interviewing the witnesses when you come in in the morning, boss."

"OK, Sergeant, do you have the weapon used?"

"That and two others, boss."

"Very good. In that case, keep it up and if you need me, give a scream. If not, I'll see you in the morning."

Steck was right. When Dunleavy came in the next morning, they were still interviewing witnesses. He spoke to an unshaven Steck, who was pouring his third cup of two-hour-old coffee and checked that the chain of custody for the weapons was done. He was looking in through the small window at the witness interrogation going on in room number one where he saw Melvin Peters shaking his head and Detective Dickie Coelho shoving a legal pad and a pencil across the table at him.

Dunleavy waved Steck over. The shadow eyed detective carried papers in one hand and his coffee in the other as he looked into the small room with his chief.

"What have you got on this guy, Danny?" Dunleavy said, pointing with this thumb through the wire reinforced window.

"Uhhh," Steck said, looking at the sheets in his hand, "Melvin Peters, age 20, picked up running away from the scene by Russo and Croom. So far, denying he saw anything. You know him, Chief?"

"Yeah, he just got out of Fishkill. Was doing a one-to-three-year stint in the Nate Harwood murder and got conditional release."

"Well, looks like he's headed back, boss. Shouldn't be hangin' out with known criminals."

Dunleavy rubbed his chin. "Let me talk to Coelho, Danny." Steck nodded and knocked on the door. Both occupants looked up, Melvin wincing. Coelho came outside and shook hands with his commander.

"Good morning, Chief," Coelho said, straightening his tie. "What do you need?"

Dunleavy looked into the room where Melvin held the pencil hovering over the legal pad. "What have you got on this guy, Dickie?"

"Not much, Chief. Denies he saw anything, claims he was headed home. Patrol picked him up running away from the scene."

Dunleavy briefed the detective on Melvin's history and clapped him on the shoulder. "Go get some coffee, Richard, and I'll talk to this guy."

Dunleavy entered the room and closed the door quietly. Melvin lowered his eyes and tapped the legal pad with the pencil.

"Melvin Peters," Dunleavy said. Melvin grabbed the pencil in both hands. "Picked up running away from a murder scene after leaving a house party. Known felons in attendance at said house party."

Melvin snapped the pencil in two.

"It's a parole violation, Melvin, plain and simple..."

"I wasn't—" Melvin said.

"And you won't be going back to Fishkill, either, Melvin. You'll probably be headed to Attica... or Elmira."

Melvin shook his head.

"Tell me what happened Melvin, I might be able to help... if you're straight with me."

Melvin crushed the top sheet of paper on the legal pad.

"If I leave this room and haven't heard what you saw, what you were doing, you'll be back on the bus to prison this afternoon."

Melvin bit his lower lip as someone in the hallway shouted, "Take him down to the holding cell, we'll book him with the rest," as one of the other partiers was removed in handcuffs.

"Your aunt and uncle probably wonder what happened to you Melvin. What do you think they'll say when they find out?"

"All right, all right, Lieutenant. I was at the party. I was leaving, OK? It was before curfew. I had time to get home before curfew. I was upstairs and the windows were open. There was a crash, there was shouting, and there were shots. By the time we got to the window, it had already happened. Everybody headed down the stairs to see. I knew I had to get out of there, so I ran." He clenched his fists. "That's the truth Lieutenant, I took off through the backyards and I didn't see nothing."

Dunleavy leaned back against the door, hands in pockets. "All right, Melvin. I want you to write down just what you told me for Detective Coelho." He opened the door and stopped. "I'm going to check what you said. If it's not true, I'll know and you'll be back on the bus to prison this afternoon. If it is true, I may be able to work something out. We'll see..."

"It's all true, Lieutenant. All of it."

"Oh, one more thing, Melvin. I read in your parole report that you did woodworking, restored furniture in Fishkill. Is that true?"

Melvin looked up, puzzled. "Yeah, I worked in the cabinetmaking shop when I was there..."

Dunleavy nodded and closed the door.

78.

Sitting at his desk, Dunleavy looked at the legal pad and noted Melvin's good handwriting and paragraph form. He even noted where Melvin had crossed out a misspelling of the word "stairway" and corrected it. *How the hell did this kid get involved with this bullshit?* he wondered.

Dunleavy looked up at the light rap on the door, and waved Steck and Coelho in.

"Well, Dickie, what's your policeman's intuition tell you about this Peters kid?"

"He's got a record, boss, but I don't figure him for one of these Python lowlifes."

"His story match up?"

"Yeah, it does," Coelho said, rubbing his rapidly bearding chin. "His story matches up with several of the others, and we kept them all separate from the start."

Dunleavy nodded and smiled, noting his procedures were being followed by his detectives.

"The evidence against Big Snake looks solid without this guy?" he asked Steck.

"Got him cold, boss. We've got the gun, he tested positive for gunshot residue on his hands, we've got his car and the victim's in the impound lot. Witnesses won't say he did it, but they place him at the scene."

"OK, then. Perhaps we could spare Mr. Peters from returning to prison for the time being, eh?"

Now it was Coelho's turn to smile. "I think with what we've got hanging over him, he'd probably help us."

"All right, then here's the way we'll play it. We bring him in, and I mention the possibility of his not going back to the pen this time. You grit your teeth and shake your head, letting him know what a bad idea you think it is…"

79.

BUFFALO POLICE HEADQUARTERS, 1980

Detective Coelho left the interrogation room shaking his head and muttering about coddling low-lifes, but his growling turned to chuckling when he had shut the door.

"The chief has got another one on the line," Coelho told Steck, who nodded.

Inside the interrogation room, Dunleavy sat down at the table directly across from Melvin, his blues eyes unblinking, his hands folded in front of him. Melvin squirmed in the plastic chair.

Dunleavy held up his left index finger. "You know one phone call from me to Mr. Herman and you're back to prison, don't you Melvin?"

Melvin nodded.

"And, even worse, the last thing you want is to be known as a snitch in the neighborhood."

Melvin held his breath and nodded.

"So here's how it works. There's no paperwork, nothing official in the records. The only ones who know are you and me," he said, pointing first to Melvin, then at his own heart.

"I've never told anyone, not even a judge, about any of my C.I.s," Dunleavy said, avoiding the use of the word *informant.* "But if you take advantage, try something cute..." he turned his hands out, palms up.

Dunleavy put his business card in front of Melvin. When Melvin tried to pick it up, Dunleavy put his finger on it.

"Uh-uh. Memorize the numbers written there to get in touch with me. Nothing, and I mean nothing with our names on it passes between us." After a few moments, Melvin nodded and Dunleavy picked up the card and put it back in the small card case he carried in his jacket pocket.

"All right, then, we understand each other. Now, here's what you've got to do…"

When he was done explaining, Dunleavy left the room and talked to Coelho in the hallway. Melvin watched while Dunleavy put on his hat and Coelho shook his head.

That hat, Melvin thought. *I know that hat. When mom got killed! That's it! Dunleavy's the cop who brought me to stay at Bernie and Erica's back then!* Melvin thought about that as Coelho let him go and all the cops gave him nasty looks. *He knows all about me from then,* he thought, riding the bus back to the projects.

80.

DOUGLASS TOWER PROJECTS, 1980

When Melvin got back to the apartment, it was one in the afternoon. Aunt Erica was sitting in her chair in the parlor, wringing a handkerchief and crying quietly. Uncle Bernie was in the kitchen, hands in pockets looking out the window. They both turned as Melvin came through the door, closing it silently behind him. Aunt Erica jumped up and hugged him.

"Melvin, Melvin, we were so worried! Are you all right, son?" she said.

"Where the hell have you been, boy? Your aunt is terrified something happened to you." Uncle Bernie said.

"It's OK, folks, it's OK," Melvin said. "I was just in the wrong place at the wrong time, is all, but it's all straight now…"

"We heard about the shooting over on Archie Street…"

"I've been praying all morning you weren't mixed up in that, Melvin…"

"It's going to be OK. Lt. Dunleavy knows I wasn't involved and got me outta there…"

Erica and Bernie looked at each other. They remembered the policeman who brought Melvin to them all those years ago.

"Praise Jesus," Erica said.

"Boy, you got to stay home nights from now on," Bernie said.

"You must be hungry, Melvin," Erica said. Let me fix you some pancakes."

When they had eaten, Melvin went to bed. "I've been up all night, but I'll be going out looking for a job tomorrow," he assured them, the names of the antique shops over on Ashland in his head.

81.

THE WEST SIDE, 1980

It took a while to get in touch with the people who ran the antique shops around Ashland and Lexington on the West Side, and Melvin got a number of suspicious looks from the locals as he knocked on doors and left notes. Only one of the shops was open during the week, the rest being run by retirees or women opening on weekends or sometimes in the evenings. One couple looked shocked when Melvin came into their store, the woman standing right by the phone the entire time he spoke to her shaking husband. Another woman couldn't do enough for him but said she didn't need any help. *Yeah, I know, lady, you used to volunteer sometimes at a school on the East Side and think Martin Luther King was wonderful,* Melvin thought.

Melvin was looking in the window of The Antique Depot when he heard a white voice behind him.

"What do you want here, kid?"

Melvin turned to see a white man with graying blonde hair in a blue blazer and khakis looking at him with narrowed eyes.

"I'm looking for work, sir," Melvin answered. *This is the guy Dunleavy wants me to keep an eye on.*

"What kind of work?" Lovejoy said, arms folding across his chest.

"I can repair furniture. Refinish it too."

"Uh huh."

"I've done moving, too."

"Where'd you learn about furniture?" Lovejoy said, looking Melvin up and down.

"Uh, vo-tech school."

"Which one?"

"Emerson."

"Did you have Mr. Roney in wood shop there?"

"Yes sir."

"Bullshit, kid, I went to Emerson and Mr. Roney's been gone for years." Pointing at Melvin's shoes, Lovejoy said, "Those are jailhouse issue shoes if I ever seen them."

Melvin dropped his head and hesitated. *Dunleavy wants me to keep an eye on this guy or it might be back to jail.* "You're right, sir. I did a little over a year. I learned in Fishkill."

"I figured. Well, tell you what," he said, opening up the shop door and leading Melvin inside. Pointing at a battered telephone stand, he said, "Let's see what you can do with this." Melvin picked it up, and Lovejoy led Melvin into the back room, where he pointed out where all the finishes, sandpaper and tools were neatly organized.

"Everything you need is back here. I'm going across the street to get something to eat. When I come back, I'll check out what you've done. You do OK, I might have some more work for you." Holding up his index finger and tilting his chin up, he added, "I'll pay you three bucks an hour, but don't fuck the dog on this, kid, you'll regret it," and he turned and walked out towards the tavern across the street.

Looking around, Melvin smelled the odor of stains and sawdust, and picked out some medium grit sandpaper to start with, thinking, *Another white bastard who wants control over me. We'll see,* he thought, *We'll see.*

Lovejoy chuckled to himself as he went up the stairs into Flynn's.

He'll fix up that phone stand Z wanted done for Strazzo's wife. And, when it's done, I'll tell Strazzo this Black kid did it.

When Lovejoy came back across the street, he belched and looked at the smooth coat of stain Melvin had put on the telephone bench.

"Wha'd you use to sand it?" he said, picking his teeth with a toothpick.

"100 grit paper," Melvin answered.

"What's next?"

"I figure, sand it down again with a fine grit, refinish it. Then one more time with steel wool, one more coat of stain and it'll be good."

Lovejoy looked at him with penetrating eyes under nearly closed lids and just a hint of a smile.

Looks just like the guys in the joint when they were about to pull one over on you, Melvin thought.

"OK, kid, c'mon back tomorrow at nine sharp. I got some more work for you. Now I gotta lock up," he said, turning towards the front door.

"Uh, what about my pay?"

"Oh, yeah," Lovejoy said with a bigger smile. He looked at his watch, said "Close enough," pulled out three singles and handed them to Melvin as they went out. "If this works out, maybe we can get you to do some moving for me, too… By the way, what's your name, kid?"

"Melvin. Melvin Peters."

"All right, Melvin Peters. Be here at nine, no later, and I'll show you what needs to be done," and he got in a metallic blue Lincoln Town Car at the curb and drove off. Melvin watched the shiny car hum off, then started walking towards Elmwood to catch the bus.

82.

ALLENTOWN, THE WEST SIDE, 1980

Sanchez walked up Virginia Street, past the Calle Virginia sign that served as a gateway to his neighborhood and slid into the narrow alley between Immaculate Conception school and church on Elmwood. The Italian sat in his Cadillac flicking ashes off his cigarette onto the pavement, watching the goateed Dominican from the parking lot.

"Hey, *chico*," Squalo said. "You Roberto's friend? The guy works in the kitchen at Roseland?"

Sanchez nodded, but didn't come from between the old red brick buildings. Dropping the cigarette, Squalo turned his palm up.

"You wanna do this thing or not?"

Sanchez nodded.

"Listen up then."

Sanchez nodded.

"All right, *chico*, here's how this works…"

"My name is Sanchez."

"Great—Chico Sanchez. Over there is School 46," he said, pointing across the street. "You know it?"

"I know it."

"When I drive away, you bring your package over to the front of School 46, and you go knock on the little door on the Edward Street side. Somebody will open the door and you give him the package. *Capiche?*"

"I got it."

"One of my guys will look it over, make sure it's all there. When he lets us know it's right, we put your package behind the dumpster, underneath the cross on the wall, right there," Squalo said, indicating the green dumpster by the wall of the Catholic school. "Got it?"

"Si, I got it."

"All right, then. Roberto says you're OK. You do this right and we can do business again. If not, we're gonna burn down Virginia Street. You understand?"

Sanchez nodded, thinking, *You arrogant prick.*

"From now on, you deal with Enzo. All right?" and with that, Squalo drove away.

83.

THE EAST SIDE, 1980

Melvin called Kisha around six, hoping she'd be home from work then. She had a nine to five secretary job downtown at an insurance company and her own place now with two other girls, Toni and Belinda. He'd called before and left messages on the answering machine, wondering if she was home and just stiffing him. Or the other girls weren't giving her the messages. The machine's message started with "This is Toni…"

Then "This is Kisha…"

And "Bee here too…"

Then Toni finished the message, "We're busy right now, leave a message," and then laughter and The Isleys' "Don't Say Goodnight" playing in the background.

He was just about to hang up as the message ended and the machine beeped. *Don't leave a message, can't let this girl think I'm desperate.* Then she picked up.

"Hello?"

"Kisha!" *Damn. Shouldn't sound so excited. Gotta cool out.*

"Oh, hello, Melvin. I haven't heard from you since the party over on Archie Street. I heard the cops got you."

"Yeah, but they kicked me loose. I told 'em I was good on the curfew and they didn't have any reason to hold me."

"Well, that's good. They held some folks all night long and busted the Snake big time. What'll happen to him?"

"Shit, I dunno. They got him pretty solid." *C'mon girl, forget that shit.* "How's your new place?"

"Ohh, it's just fine. You know Belinda and Toni, right?"

"Oh yeah. Bee and me went to Bennett."

"Oh, that's right. You were the smart ones went to Bennett."

"Yeah, but you're the one with the downtown job now, girl. How's that working?"

"Pretty good, filing and typing and answering the phone, you know. The hours suck but the pay ain't bad. How about you?"

"I'm working over across town, refinishing furniture. I'm thinking about going back to school, maybe take accounting."

"That's good. You got regular hours over there?"

"Yeah, pretty much. Work on the weekends sometimes."

"This weekend?"

"Naw, I got it off. I was thinking we could go over to Mattie's for dinner Saturday night."

"Ooooh, Mattie's. I want to try their ox tail!"

"Well, all right. I'll come by and get you around six."

Yes! he thought as he hung up. *Mattie's is nice, and there won't be any trouble in there to interrupt us.*

They were just finishing dessert when he checked the watch that Uncle Bernie gave him. *Damn it! I got to get home in twenty minutes.*

"Something wrong, Melvin?"

"Curfew. I gotta be back home soon or they might violate me."

"Shee-it, and I was going to ask you to come see my apartment," she said, lowering her eyes.

Dammit, dammit, dammit! Herman and Dunleavy's voices sounded in his head, and memories of the barred doors slamming shut in Elmira tensed him up.

Melvin awoke the next morning before the alarm went off for work. He looked around at the comfortable room, smelled bacon cooking in the kitchen, then looked out the window at the other high rise ghetto across the walkway. *How do I get out of this mess? Cops. Parole officers. Pythons. Some crook in the antique store. What the hell is his game, anyway? Got to be something bad for homicide to want to track him. That stare of his. Always sizing you up. I just want to live a normal life! My life's been fucked over one way or another since dad took off... What if I just stay right here in the apartment, not go anywhere? Yeah, I have to see Herman again tomorrow. He'll want to know if I've been going to work... and I've got to check in with Dunleavy, too. I heard Kelvin and the rest of them jitterbugging outside with the Madadors last night after I came in, too. A couple of gunshots even. Everywhere I turn, trouble. Saturday! That's right! I'm going to see Kisha Saturday on her day off. All day maybe, don't have to worry about curfew until that night.*

Thinking about curfews, Melvin wondered how Anton was doing. *Must be getting close to getting out,* he thought. *I wonder if he's been moved.*

Going out into the kitchen, he saw Uncle Bernie reading the paper.

"Hey, Unc," he said, scratching his head.

"Well, good morning Melvin. Your aunt's got breakfast almost ready." *Every day, they're up before dawn, even though they're both retired.*

"Hey, Unc," Melvin asked. "Can I make a long distance phone call? I'll pay you back. I just want to check on a friend of mine."

"Why sure, Melvin. You go right ahead, and don't worry about the money son... unless you're planning on calling Tokyo or someplace."

"Thanks, Unc, I won't be long."

Melvin dialed the number he'd mailed to his Aunt and Uncle when he first went to Elmira.

"Elmira Correctional Facility."

"Uh, hi. I'm trying to get in touch with an inmate there? His name is Anton Maudit."

"I cannot connect you with the inmate now sir. He may be able to call you if you are on his approved phone list."

"How do I get on that list?

"Are you a family member?"

"Uh… yes. I'm his brother and I live in Buffalo now."

"I see. I cannot connect you with the inmate now, but if you are on the approved list…"

"Well, can you tell me if he's in the facility at least?"

"What was his name again sir?"

"Anton Maudit. Former residence, Bronx, NY."

"Let me see, sir. I'll have to put you on hold while I check."

Anton waited in silence, hoping he didn't get disconnected. The operator came back after five minutes.

"Sir?"

"Yes?"

"Anton Maudit is here. He is currently in the general population. Would you like to know how you get on the approved call list?"

Oh, God, no, Melvin thought. *Hang in there, Anton, you'll be out soon.*

"Sir?"

"No, no thank you," Melvin said, and hung up.

84.

FILLMORE AVENUE, 1980

Rakestraw came into the back of the shop and asked, "Can you drive, kid?" shaking the keys to a white van.

"Yeah, I gotta license," Melvin said.

"Good," he said, tossing him the keys. "We're headed to this old bank over on Fillmore. Closed down a while ago, got sold. The new owner wants to unload the president of the bank's old desk. No idea what he's got. Make some change on this for sure."

They drove down the declining commercial street, where every other store was closed, and half the houses were for sale. "Used to be all Polish around here," Rakestraw said, noting all the Black pedestrians. Coming to a two story red brick structure, Rakestraw pointed to the parking lot behind it, where a sign, half hanging off a pole said, "Savings and Loan Parking Only."

They hauled the desk out to the van, locked it up and Rakestraw said, "Let's look around the rest of the place, see if there's anything else worth snatching." There were a few old chairs which Rakestraw examined and rejected, remarking, "Junk," and a few carpets he kicked over saying, "Trash. Couldn't get five bucks for the lot."

As they were at the back door, they spotted a guy trying to work a Slim Jim into the van's passenger door.

"Gimme that box cutter I gave you," Rakestraw said. Melvin

handed it over. "Stay put," he said, pulling a .22 revolver out of his belt. Melvin watched as Rakestraw slipped outside and put the pistol to the thief's head and forced him to the ground. Melvin came outside just as Rakestraw stepped on the man's hand and slashed it with the box cutter, cutting deep enough to sever tendons.

"Goddamn man, what the fuck?" the thief screamed, and Rakestraw kicked him in the head.

"Get outta here, you son-of-a -bitch! Think you can fuck with my van?" he said, waving the box cutter in the thief's face. The man grabbed his hand and ran off.

"Let's get the hell out of here, Melvin. This neighborhood's turned to shit," he said, wiping the box cutter off with a rag and giving it back to Melvin. He kept the pistol at his side until they were in the van and moving. Melvin said nothing the rest of the trip, and Rakestraw left after they lugged the desk back into the shop.

85.

DERBY, NY, 1980

When Melvin was eating breakfast the next day, the phone rang. Aunt Erica answered it, then said quietly, "It's for you, Melvin. I think it's your boss." Melvin got up and went to the wall phone.

"We got some furniture to pick up out in the country today, Melvin. It'll take two guys. You got any friends who want to make a few bucks?"

"Sure. I can get someone."

"Good. Meet me at the shop at nine."

Melvin thought for a while, trying to think of somebody without a record or a job. He settled on Jimmy, a friend who lived down in the Perry Street projects. It took some time to explain to him how to get to the shop, but that done, he went off to work.

Rakestraw was waiting for them.

"All right, guys, here's the plan. It's Jimmy, right? OK, Jimmy, you ride with Melvin in the van and I'll drive out with you in my car, show you the way. You ever been to Derby before?" Both movers shook their heads.

"No problem, just follow me. We're headed out to a house down on the lake. Family wants to unload the furniture of their old summer house. They're getting out of Dodge and want to sell everything."

Heading down Route 5 along the lakefront, the two project boys said little, just stared out at the water, the boats and the sunlight reflecting off the waves. When they got close to Derby, they rolled the windows down and breathed in the fresh air and admired the green trees lining the side of the roads.

"Nice out here," Jimmy said.

Why would anyone want to move away from here? Melvin thought.

They followed Rakestraw down a gravel driveway to a yellow and white one and a half story frame house with a screened in porch surrounded by pine trees.

"We might be the first Black people out here," Jimmy said.

"Why do you think Rakestraw's here?" Melvin said out of the corner of his mouth.

Rakestraw watched as they hauled the furniture out to the van and he talked to the woman who owned the place.

"It's just so depressing around Buffalo these days," she said. "Tom has sold the business to a trading company, and they're selling everything to some Chinese concern."

"Uh huh," Rakestraw said, as Melvin and Jimmy carried a loveseat past them.

"Oh, there goes our old loveseat. We got that when we bought the place so many years ago."

"Hmm," Rakestraw said. "Hold up a second, fellas. He walked over to the loveseat and brushed his hand over the upholstery. "See that, Mrs. Darwin? The upholstery on this loveseat is in bad shape. I don't know if I can get it clean or not. Might have to replace it. I doubt if I'll make anything on it with all the work it'll take."

"Well, we certainly won't need it out in Tucson. You just give me your estimate for the lot and Tom and I will look it over."

When they were just about finished, Rakestraw gave Melvin and Jimmy Pepsis, which they drank on the last two wicker chairs on the porch as the sun quietly set over the pointed treetops of the evergreens.

"I love that smell. That smell of the pine trees," Melvin said, looking around.

"Beats the projects by a mile," Jimmy said.

"As bad as the real estate market has been," Mrs. Darwin said, "we might even consider renting the place."

They drove back to the city. Rakestraw was sure he'd knocked the price down on the furniture by at least half, and Melvin wondered what the rent would be on the house.

86.

DOUGLAS TOWER PROJECTS, 1980

Melvin looked at the church calendar hanging in the kitchen and thought, *Anton should be out by now, even if he had to do the whole stretch.* Going into his room, he dug through the dresser drawer full of junk and found the phone number in the Bronx where he said he'd be.

"Uncle Bernie," he said, "I'm going to make a long distance call to New York. Just let me know how much it is and I'll pay you back."

"Don't worry about that, Melvin. This to your friend in the Bronx you talked about?"

"Yeah, he should be home by now."

"Go ahead, boy, don't worry about it. Talk to your friend."

Melvin dialed the number and got a recording. "The number you have reached is out of service." He tried again, making sure he got the number right, but got the same result. Next, he called Elmira.

"Elmira Correctional Facility."

Melvin gave them Anton's name. The operator came back, saying, "That inmate is no longer here."

"Can you tell me when he was released?"

"That inmate is no longer here."

"What does that mean? Has he been released? Transferred? C'mon, what happened to him?"

"That's all the information I can give you, sir."

Melvin hung up, wondering how to find Anton. He could be anywhere in New York.

After hanging up, he thought about it and remembered Dunleavy had tracked him when he got out of Fishkill. He dialed the Homicide commander's office.

"Dunleavy here."

"Lieutenant, this is Melvin. I was wondering if you could help me with something?"

"You're not in trouble again, are you?"

"No, no, I'm fine. See, there's this friend of mine I was inside with, and he should've got out by now, but his phone's disconnected and Corrections won't tell me anything."

"You're not supposed to associate with convicts, Melvin."

"This is the guy who I kept from killing himself, Lieutenant. I just want to see how he's doing. He lives in New York, I won't be hanging out with him or anything."

After a long pause, Dunleavy said, "All right, Melvin, give me his name and any other information you have and I'll see what I can do."

That night, the phone rang and Aunt Erica answered.

"Melvin, it's for you."

Melvin answered and turned to the wall while Erica washed dishes.

"Yes?"

"Melvin, it's Lieutenant Dunleavy."

"Did you find him? Anton, I mean?"

"Yes. I've got some bad news. After he was in the mental health unit for a while, they returned him to the general population at Elmira. He killed himself two weeks later. I'm sorry."

Melvin hung up. *A few more months. All he had to do was hang on for a few more months. I should've written him. They wouldn't let me call him. Maybe I could've...*

"Are you all right, Melvin?" Erica asked.

"I'll be OK, Aunt Erica." Tears came down his cheeks and he went to his room before anyone saw.

87.

NEW YORK STATE THRUWAY, CORFU, NY, 1980

Twitch pulled into a gas station and called the number he knew well.

"Hello?" the voice challenged.

"Enzo? What are you doing there?"

"I'm taking care of the boss. What the fuck do you think? You took off and nobody's here to take care of the old man."

"Is he OK?"

"Of course he's OK. His daughter comes in to fix his meals like always and Ralph and me take care of the business."

"Oh, good. I was worried."

"Where the hell are you anyway? You vanished after the trial. What the fuck, you got off, didn't you?"

"Yeah, I got some business to take care of, want to stay away until things quiet down some. The cops are pretty mad…" *I don't get this*, Twitch thought. *Aren't these guys looking for me because of the bombing? Dunleavy…*

"You asshole, you watch the news?"

"I'm, uhhh, outta town, Enzo. I got business…"

"Your house burned down, you dipshit. Did you know that?"

"Huh?"

"Your house caught on fire, you asshole. Burned to the ground.

The cops and the arson guys are all over it, and you didn't know?"

"No, I haven't seen the Buffalo papers or the news…"

"Look, idiot. You better talk to Ralph, get all this shit straight. It coulda been the same people… with his house."

Squalo doesn't think I bombed his house? What about Dunleavy's threat?

"You hear me, you spastic? You better talk to Squalo. You know how."

"What…"

"That's all I'm gonna say," and Enzo hung up.

Squalo and Enzo were sitting in the café when the pay phone rang. Nobody moved to answer it. Both men listened to the rings. When it stopped, Enzo looked at his cousin.

"Four rings, let's go," Squalo said, and they both went out the back door and drove off. They double parked in front of the liquor store on Niagara Street and walked through the store briskly, brushing past the weaving man dropping coins on the counter next to the bottle of fortified wine. Nodding to the elderly man in the ratty cardigan behind the counter, they went back into the storeroom where the walls were mostly exposed plaster lath and the place smelled of rotting cardboard. There was a scarred wooden desk with liquor and wine promotional signs stacked up on it and Squalo dropped himself in a rolling swivel chair as Enzo closed the door. The chair's bearings crunched under Squalo's bulk and tilted to the side.

"What the fuck?" Squalo said, grasping the seat and straightening it. "We gotta tell that old fool to get a decent chair for us," he said, adjusting the stained cushion. He looked around the room and jutting his chin towards a stack of whiskey cases against the wall said, "Grab us a bottle of V.O., Cuz." Enzo was ripping the cardboard lid open when the phone rang.

"Hello?" Squalo said.

"It's me," Twitch said, closing the door to the phone booth at the rest stop on the Thruway.

"What the fuck are you doin', you asshole?"

"I got business, out of town."

"Look, Enzo's been taking care of things at the old man's house. He can't be doing that. He's got important business. Whaddayou scared?"

"Enzo said my house burned down. The cops are mad. Dunleavy…"

"Fuck him, that Irish bastard. Fuck all them cops. I know who did your house, I know who did my house, and he's gonna get his."

"There's something else. You know the old garage on Niagara, the one Galbo used to run near Auburn?"

"Yeah, what about it?"

"I saw the FBI pick Z up in the lot there. Took him away, took his car, too."

"When the fuck was this?"

"Weeks ago. I been trying to get hold of you since."

"How do you know?"

"I saw it. Right there. I was coming down Niagara and they pulled him over, cuffed him and took him and his car someplace north."

"I thought you were outta town?"

"I had to… get some money I had. In a deposit box."

"That fucking fat fuck…"

"He's a rat for sure, Squalo."

There was silence for several seconds. Then Squalo spoke.

"Look, you little weasel, I gotta have you looking after the old man. I'm gonna be the boss from now on, I just gotta get a couple of things taken care of. You'll know, believe me."

"But, my house…"

"Forget it, stay in the old man's house. Get your spastic ass back here," and hung up. He looked over at Enzo, who had heard everything.

"I knew it had to be Strazzo or one of his boys. That fucker's still mad over the tanker truck deal thirty-five years ago. And Z? If the Feds didn't hold him, he's talking. We gotta act now."

"What about Twitch?"

"Lemme think about that..."

Twitch stared at the phone, thinking as the dial tone hummed. *He thinks Strazzo did it? Maybe Dunleavy didn't say anything... Squalo always hated Dunleavy, maybe he didn't believe him...* Twitch shook his head and went into the Holiday House and bought the papers.

As Squalo pushed himself out of the battered chair he said, "You think the lawyer's right? You think they'll make them take all those wiretaps out and we can go back to using our phones?"

Slapping Squalo on the back as they exited the liquor store, "That's what we pay the shyster for isn't it?" Enzo said, tossing the whiskey bottle in the back seat.

Jerking his thumb behind them, Squalo said, "It'll beat running around like this to be able to talk, that's for damn sure." He wheeled out into traffic, cutting off a guy in a station wagon who slammed on his brakes, blowing his horn and cursing at them.

88.

THE WEST SIDE, 1980

Squalo threw away his cigarette as he walked out of the back door of the bar on Grant Street when Enzo pulled up in the lot in a rusted out ten-year-old Ford F-100 pickup truck.

"What the fuck is this?" Squalo said. "Some kind of Beverly Hillbillies bullshit?"

"Don't worry, it's perfect for what we're doing out there."

"You got what we need?"

"Absolutely," he said, nodding to the shopping bag on the floor. Squalo bent over and opened it wide, pursing his lips in admiration at the two Berretta automatic pistols.

"Looks good. You check 'em?"

"Naturally. Doug that just got out of the Army got me these. Says the Army's going to use 'em to replace their .45s. Definitely more accurate."

"Good, good. He should be leaving the dinner in about an hour, the sun will be down. It'll be perfect," Squalo said, racking a round into the chamber.

89.

F.B.I. SOG SQUAD OFFICE, AMHERST, 1980

Perez was monitoring the tracers and the microphones from one of the rolling desk chairs with his hands behind his head when Mehltretter came back into the warehouse with dinner.

"A Whopper with cheese, fish sandwich, regular fries, apple pie and large Coke, right?" the agent said, laying the paper-wrapped food on the folding table behind Perez, sliding an empty pizza box and fast food cups out of the way.

"I am so sick of listening to these idiots talk about hockey," Perez said.

"Nothing doing in the café or the union hall?"

"Nah. The boss says they're probably onto us there. We probably won't catch anything unless they get stupid or drunk."

"Where are our two big shot cars?"

"Squalo's is sitting in his driveway and Strazzo's is out on Grand Island. We heard he was going out to dinner out there. Hey, look at this, he's moved some, he's out in the middle of nowhere. Been there for a while. Whaddaya think?" Perez said, squeezing a package of vinegar onto his fries.

"Let's call the boss, see what he says," Mehltretter said, chomping down on a chicken sandwich and dialing the senior agent's beeper. A few minutes and most of a rapidly devoured meal later, the phone rang on the table.

"Amherst Liquidators."

"What's up?" Shea said.

"Boss, we got Strazzo out on Grand Island, but it looks like he's left the restaurant. He's out on Love Road between a couple of fields. Been there for about an hour."

"Get hold of Amodeo now. Tell him to come in no matter what he's doing. Get hold of Silverstein and a crew from downtown and tell them to meet me at the location on Love Road. Yeah, and call the sheriffs out there too."

90.

HORSEHEADS, NY, 1980

Twitch got to the railroad car diner with the awning before the sun came up and parked around the back. He picked up the papers from Buffalo in the boxes out front and sat in a booth where he could watch the front and the side doors. The waitress signaled with the coffee pot from behind the counter, and he nodded, then sat down spreading the papers on the Formica topped table. When he saw the headline in the *Courier*, he clutched both sides and held it. The waitress noticed he was muttering the paper's words as she turned over the cup and poured the coffee.

"The F.B.I., Erie County Sheriffs and New York State Police responded to what appears to be an underworld related double murder on Love Road on Grand Island last night around 9:30 p.m. Grant Strozzare was found shot to death in his car on Love Road east of Baseline. Another Buffalo man, Zeno LaPancia was found a short time later by police in a field alongside the road. Strozzare, known as "Strazzo," reputedly a prominent organized crime figure in Buffalo, and LaPancia, also identified by police as a mob associate, had attended a dinner earlier in the evening at the popular Herb and Del's restaurant on the Island for the retirement of local politician…" Twitch looked at the waitress and said, "I gotta make a phone call…"

Twitch had to get four dollars' worth of change and spent most of it trying to get hold of Squalo while the waitress gave him impatient looks while people waited for the booth. When Squalo finally called him back, he turned away and covered the receiver with his hand.

"Look, Twitch, c'mon in and talk to me. Everything's been taken care of. I got tickets to the Sabres game tomorrow night, we can talk there at the Aud. Yeah, my regular tickets in the Reds. Meet me at the entrance. If you're a good boy, I'll even buy you a bag of Buffalo's Best Peanuts, you *chooch*. All right? I'll see you there."

Squalo hung up and turned to Enzo, rocks glass of V.O. in hand. "Now, we just take care of a few other minor details, eliminate a few weak links, and everybody knows I'm the man now. Cheers."

91.

F.B.I. SOG SQUAD OFFICE, AMHERST, 1980

Leo brought a package of Eight O'Clock Coffee with him to the industrial park, figuring some decent coffee might loosen them up.

Silverstein tapped Shea on the shoulder. The senior agent turned in his chair, hit a button and took off the earphones.

"Chief. Welcome. I've got some of the information from the sheriff and the troopers on the Strazzo shooting here," Shea said, handing Dunleavy a manila envelope file with 8" x 10" black and white photographs.

"They wanted him dead, that's for sure," Dunleavy said, turning the photographs to different angles.

"The Firearms Unit says 9 mm bullets, two guns used. Maybe stolen new army issue sidearms."

"Ach," Dunleavy said, looking at a photo of Z's body in the field.

"Yeah, they worked him over pretty good before they killed him."

Handing Shea back a particularly gory photograph of Z's remains, Dunleavy said, "You know what this means, right?"

"They usually only do that to informants."

"Was he talking to you?"

"He was cooperating. I have no idea how they found out…"

"I wonder what he told them before he died."

Looking down, Shea said, "We've been following some of Squalo's boys on their comings and goings from Jersey Street. They're a slippery bunch. Cut people off, go the wrong way on one-way streets, park wherever they feel like it. We've got tracers on Squalo and Enzo's cars now, and we know they were parked at their houses that night. We did find out another thing though, from another place we have wired—he's not mad at your boy Twitch, wants him to come in and meet him at a Sabres game. Still wants him to take care of the old man."

Leo reflected on that information and thought about what he'd give the Federal agent in return. "How are you doing with the rest of Strazzo's crew?"

"Not so good. We've got the union office wired on Franklin Street, but they keep their cards pretty close to the vest when they're in there."

"Yeah, they know you guys are probably listening. Most of the decisions get made over at Fat Sam's before the meetings. That's where you want to listen."

"How the hell did you learn that, Chief?"

"A leprechaun whispered it in my ear," he said, thinking of Jimmy Devine, one of the local's shop stewards. Leo and Adele had run into him at a South Park High School reunion at Danny's, and many beers later with the women out on the dance floor, Jimmy had started complaining about the mob guys running his local.

"Those bastards," Jimmy slurred, "make all the decisions before they come to the meetings. Oh yeah, they get together over at Fat Sam's at five for dinner, so everything's decided before they come to the meeting at the hall at seven. Me and some of the other guys, you know them, Tommy Fabrizzi and Larry Czup, we start hootin' and hollerin' at the meeting, but either there's not enough guys to pass the motion, or there's some friggin' rule, or we're outta order, or some other bullshit…"

92.

LOVEJOY, THE EAST SIDE, 1980

"You guys finished?" Rakestraw said to the three men standing by the van in the driveway on Moreland.

"Just about," Melvin said. "I got to lock up the cottage before we go. The credenza, the dining room table and six chairs, right?"

"Right. Get them set up over at the shop in the middle room. The client'll be by tomorrow to take a look at them. Make sure you give them a good polish when you get over there, Melvin."

"Yeah, OK, I'll just lock this place up then."

"Nah, I'll get it Melvin. You guys go on ahead. Just make sure they're cleaned up good for when I meet up with the client tomorrow morning at 10:00."

"OK."

Melvin checked the straps securing the furniture in the van while the two other guys hopped in the cab. As he climbed up in the driver's seat, he saw Rakestraw put the keys in his pocket and enter the cottage. In the mirror, he saw Rakestraw bent over through the partially curtained window. *What's he pulling up off the floor?* he thought.

When they got to the shop on Ashland Street, Melvin told the other guys to start unloading the furniture, he had to make a phone call. As he started across the street to the bar, he heard Jimmy say,

"Man, hustle up. We don't want to be doing this all ourselves."

Tony bitched, too. "Damn white ass cheapskate won't even put a phone in his shop."

Melvin went straight to the wooden phone booth by the coatroom as an older white man at the bar stared at the young Black man in work clothes.

"What's *this* all about?" the elderly man muttered as Melvin closed the booth's door. Quickly dialing Dunleavy's number, he looked at his watch. *Should still be at work. Now, if he's in his office.*

"Dunleavy here."

"Lieutenant, this is Melvin. We just picked up some furniture in the cottage and are bringing it over to the shop. Looks like he'll be around tonight, he's got a client coming in tomorrow at 10:00 to look at some stuff."

"Good, Melvin, thanks. Anything else?"

"Yeah, something a little weird. He told us to go on, he'd lock the cottage up, but when I looked back, he was inside there, bent over. Sounded like he was prying up something."

"Huh, yeah, that's a little strange. All right, if anything else happens, gimme a holler."

Dunleavy thought for a few minutes, then called the bar.

"Good evening, Flynn's."

"Tom, it's Dunleavy. Have you seen our antiques dealer friend?"

Tom turned away from the bar and spoke quietly. "Yeah, he was in last night. They're over there now, taking some furniture into his shop. Huh, yeah. I offered him two tickets to the Sabres for tonight, said he was already planning on being there, and he laughed about it. No, I don't know why. Yeah, OK, bye."

That's weird, Melvin thought as he tossed back a handful of peanuts. *He must be watching him too.* Melvin took a sip of beer and looked across the street. *I'll finish this beer, they'll be just about done carrying the credenza in by then. And it pisses off that old white man at the end of the bar, too.*

Dunleavy got on the phone again, this time calling home.

"Don't say it—something's come up and you'll be late," Adele said.

"I wanted to call before you started supper," Dunleavy said.

"Jimmy's staying downtown after school, there's a basketball game tonight. Says he'll eat at McDonald's."

"Oh, that's right. He hopes he'll run into the Beiter girl from the Mount there."

"Who are they playing?"

"Turner."

"OK, look, I shouldn't be long, just something I want to check out downtown by the Aud. How about if we go to the Parkridge Inn for dinner as long as it's just you and me?"

"All right," she sighed. After she hung up the phone, she turned up the scanner.

Lovejoy parked next to the highway pier under the Skyway where Twitch would have to pass when he parked for the hockey game. He sat in the car as the sun was going down and pulled on the cheap windbreaker and gloves he'd bought on the way into town as Herb Alpert's "Rise" played on the radio. *That's a good one,* he thought, *they don't make pop tunes like that much these days. Good one to get laid by.* He put the .22 with the silencer in one of the windbreaker's pockets and a plastic bag in the other. He slid down in the seat when he saw the red Buick drive by, Twitch looking around for an open spot. Lovejoy got out of the car and followed the Buick's taillights as Twitch found a spot closer to where the old gray warships were docked at the Naval Park. *Just right. Closer to the water.*

Lovejoy looked around as Twitch stopped the car. *No one, it's early yet,* Lovejoy thought. *He probably wants to scout around himself to see if it's safe.* He walked quickly up to the car and leveled the pistol just as Twitch opened the door.

"What the…? You son of a…" Twitch said as Lovejoy shot him twice in the chest, the silencer keeping the sound down to a muffled pop, pop. Lovejoy shoved him back over onto the driver's seat, took a quick look around, and shot Twitch once more through the eye. There wasn't much blood from the small caliber bullets, and *no one will look at this car until after the game,* Lovejoy thought, as he locked and shut the door. He stepped behind another pier, put the gun into the plastic bag from his pocket, stripped off the cheap windbreaker and gloves and put them in the bag as well. Another quick look around told him he was alone, and he started walking down towards the water, tying the corners of the plastic bag together in a knot and shaking the bag. *Plenty of weight,* he thought. *It'll go down to the bottom of the river and sink into the mud forever.*

When they were done with the furniture, Melvin took the van and dropped Jimmy and Tony off in the Perry Street projects, thinking *Rick James came out of these projects, how am I going to get out of mine?* Coming back up South Park, he saw cars starting to roll in for the hockey game and spotted Dunleavy's Dodge among them. *I wonder…* and he started to follow the car as it went under the Skyway.

His Lieutenant said Joe McAvoy had been on the job forever, and he was just about ready to retire from the force, but still, when the offer of a couple of hours of easy overtime directing traffic at the Aud came up, the veteran policeman couldn't resist. As long as he didn't have to deal with booking some obnoxious drunk that would make him late getting home, it was fine with him. When he saw Chief Dunleavy drive up in his work vehicle, and by himself at that, his cop radar switched on.

"Hello, Chief," he said, as Dunleavy rolled down the window. "Adele not coming with you this evening?"

"No, Joe, I'm just scouting around on my way home. See anything hinky going on?"

"Nah, all calm so far. Probably won't be any trouble until the beer starts kicking in later on."

"OK, Joe, just keep your eyes open and your radio turned up."

"Right," McAvoy said, wondering what brought the head of Homicide down here besides hockey. Straightening up, he saw a young Black guy driving a van around into the lot. *A Black hockey fan?* he thought. *Might be a McKegney fan, though,* thinking of the Black guy who played left wing for the Sabres. He made a mental note of the vehicle and license number.

Dunleavy spotted the red Buick and pulled up alongside. *Twitch's car.* He stepped out and glanced in the window while the car behind him blew his horn, impatient to find a parking spot. Seeing the bloodied head, he pulled out his portable radio and turned up the volume.

"Homicide 270 to radio, urgent."

"Radio, go ahead."

"Shooting in the parking lot at the Aud, under the Skyway. Red Buick, license number New York E-3786. One shot at this time."

The other driver continued blowing his horn.

"Homicide 270, repeat your message, your message was unreadable."

Joe McAvoy had heard it though and ran like he was twenty years old again towards the red Buick as Dunleavy smashed the car window with the butt of the portable radio. Opening the door, Dunleavy checked and saw the blood still leaking from one of Twitch's eyes and the other with a dilated, sightless pupil.

Just happened, he thought and looked around. In the distance he spotted a well-dressed man with graying hair walking calmly towards the water.

"What happened, Chief?" McAvoy said, breathing hard.

Dunleavy pointed with his portable radio inside the car. "One shot. Dead. The gunman may be over there, by the water. Stay here with the body and send the next units down by the Naval

Park," and he started jogging towards the water.

Adele heard part of Leo's message from the scanner, then heard the airwaves get crowded with responding units calling in. *Damn it, he's not a kid anymore, he can't be doing this,* and grabbed her rosary from the kitchen drawer where she kept the flashlight and other odds and ends.

Melvin stopped the van and saw Dunleavy get out of the car, then the other cop rushing over. When he saw Dunleavy jogging towards the water, he scanned the riverfront and spotted Rakestraw ambling along. A car beeped behind him, and he put the van in gear, heading towards the water slowly.

Lovejoy was walking along the river, heading for where it got wider and deeper when he heard the sirens. He stopped and turned. *Hmm, coming from all directions. Don't hear any air horns, must be police.* Then he spotted the fedora-wearing figure rushing towards him.

"Stop, Buffalo Police!" Dunleavy shouted as Lovejoy turned towards him.

If I toss the package now, they'll drag the river and find it. If I hang onto it, I'm dead, Lovejoy thought as he pulled the .22 out of the bag.

Dunleavy stopped, realized he had the portable radio in his hand and was going for the detective special on his hip when the bullet hit him in the shoulder. He staggered backwards and slipped on the ice as the second round went overhead, laboring to get his weapon out from under his overcoat.

Eliminate the witness, get rid of the evidence, get out of town, rushed through Lovejoy's head as he took aim at the figure struggling on the ground.

Melvin stomped on the gas pedal. He closed his eyes when he heard the crunch as the van's bumper busted Lovejoy's hip and threw him off to the side. He opened his eyes and saw Dunleavy getting to his feet, snub nosed revolver in his hand. Dunleavy walked forward and waved Melvin away.

"Bastard," Lovejoy groaned as he sat up and raised the .22. Dunleavy fired. Once, twice, three times, knocking Lovejoy back flat onto the gravel. He kicked the .22 loose from the killer's hand and looked around for the portable radio. Hearing the sirens coming now, he stopped and grabbed his shoulder, pistol still in hand. Melvin was out of the van now, and Dunleavy nodded at him, alternating a wince of pain with a smile.

93.

SHEEHAN MEMORIAL HOSPITAL, 1980

Dunleavy was just coming to after the surgery, and the first voice he heard, he didn't recognize. It definitely didn't match the face he saw, which was Adele's giving him her most concerned frown.

"It took them longer than expected," the male voice said. "The bullet twisted around in there."

"Will you shut the hell up, Zeke. His wife's here," another male voice said.

When he focused, he saw two guys in fire department sweatshirts standing behind Adele. Zeke and Aaron. Adele dismissed Zeke's comments with a wave.

"Talk all you want, boys. I've heard it all before," she said, stepping to one side so they could shake Leo's good hand.

"You did it, Chief," Zeke said. "You got him, you got the bastard. Oh, excuse me, Mrs. Dunleavy…"

Leo was too tired and doped up to explain. He pointed at a figure in the corner. "Give him the reward, he got the guy who…" everyone turned to look at Melvin.

"Take the money, Melvin… take the reward money and get the hell out of Buffalo…" Dunleavy said as he faded into unconsciousness.

94.

UNIVERSITY HEIGHTS, NORTH BUFFALO, 1980

When Adele pulled into the driveway, she saw Ceelee going into the house. After hanging up her coat, she went into the kitchen, where the girl was opening a bottle of beer.

"I thought you were coming with me to see your father in the hospital?"

"I will tonight," Ceelee said, noting her mother's look of disapproval at the bottle. "I was busy taking a test and we went out afterwards."

"What test? It's a Saturday," Adele said, raising an eyebrow.

Ceelee took a deep breath. "The entrance exam for the police department," she said.

95.

LOWER WEST SIDE, 1980

This time, Sanchez thought, *no need to call that Enzo bastard.* He drove the Oldsmobile upstate from Washington Heights, the *manteca* and coke practically busting out of the door panels. He rode right past the school where he'd met the Italian before and kept on going to Virginia Street, and then down to Tenth, where Tiburon had rented a house. It was a dump, but all he needed was a place where he could make the deals. Lobo could sit in the back yard and meet the dealers when it was nice. Roberto could watch them from upstairs with the shotgun and Rafie would meet the buyers someplace in the neighborhood and pass it out. Tomas had rented the house out in Cheektowaga to stash the dope. *Seguro. Easy. No middleman anymore.*

96.

SHEEHAN MEMORIAL HOSPITAL, 1980

As Dunleavy's eyes focused, he made out Shea and his boss Katz looking at him.

"Hello, boys," he said. "Nice to see the Feds performing the corporal works of mercy."

Katz looked quizzical.

"He's been given a lot of medications," Shea said. Then, to Dunleavy, "Amodeo and Silverstein would've stopped by, but we didn't want anybody to spot them and blow their cover."

"Ah, they're good boys you've got there," Dunleavy said. Then to Katz, "You've got to learn to trust us a little, agent in charge."

"We've got some good news, Chief," Katz said.

"You got me season tickets to the Sabres."

"No, not quite. But we got those other places you mentioned wired up and we're getting useful information from them. We should have what's left of Strazzo's boys wrapped up tight very soon."

"And Strazzo's killers?"

"Working on it, Chief, working on it," Shea said.

"Just remember…" Dunleavy said. "Just remember what Inspector Wachter told me… if you don't get 'em…"

The Federal Agents looked at each other, wondering who Inspector Wachter was.

"Try the phone, too," Dunleavy continued.

"What phone, Chief?"

"The phone in the back room of the liquor store on Niagara. They use that..." he said as he fell back to sleep.

97.

DERBY, NY, 1980

In the end, the reward money went to fund the Calabotta kids' education. Parole Officer Herman, after learning of Melvin's actions, went before the parole board with several letters from police and fire department officials and recommended an immediate discharge from early release supervision, which was granted by an amazed membership after they verified the authenticity of the letters.

Melvin, having kept a set of keys to the antique shop, kept it open seven days a week, unlike his competitors on the block, who were jealous of his zeal. Visitors wondered who the cute girl was in the tight jeans visiting him on Saturdays that he took to dinner afterwards at the tavern across the street.

Reading the paper one morning while waiting for a client in the shop, Melvin turned to the real estate pages and spotted the house out in Derby was still for sale. In fact, it was also listed for rent. *Damn, I wonder...* He called the number and drove out there, arriving early to meet Mrs. Darwin. After a slightly startled recognition, *is it because I'm Black, or because of Rakestraw,* Melvin wondered, she took him around the house again. In the upstairs hallway, he noticed part of the ceiling was discolored.

"Hmm, looks like the roof's leaking over here," he said pointing.

"O Lord, that's just what we need now," she said.

"Mrs. Darwin, I can fix that, that's not a problem. I won't even charge you to do that. But, maybe you could knock a little off the rent for us?"

"Us?" she said.

"Yeah. If I rent the place, I was planning on living here with my aunt and uncle. They're retired and would like living in the country."

"Retired you say?"

"Yes, ma'am. Uncle Bernie's retired from the American Axle plant on Delevan and Aunt Erica worked at Sisters' Hospital for over thirty years."

"Well... well, Melvin, I think we might be able to work something out if you can put down a deposit..."

Melvin kept the shop on Ashland open until he had sold everything there and in the cottage, which Dunleavy's men had torn apart searching for weapons and whatever else Lovejoy had hidden there. When dunning notices started arriving from the utility and the mortgage companies for those properties, Melvin turned out the lights, pulled down the curtains and locked the doors. He took the cash, put a two-month deposit on the house in Derby and bought a used car. After he'd moved Aunt Erica and Uncle Bernie out to the house in Derby, he drove the van and parked it over on Jefferson in Python country, left the keys in the ignition and the doors unlocked. There wasn't much in the way of jobs in the lakefront area around Derby, but he found a part time job at a hardware store further down the lake in Angola, and soon became well known as the guy to call when your summer house needed work off-season.

Erica put her plants in the ground that spring and Bernie got out his fishing pole nearly every day and headed down to the lake. Aunt Erica never ceased to remind Melvin of his good fortune at the Lord's hands, and sometimes he came in with her when he drove her to church on Sundays.

98.

BUFFALO POLICE HEADQUARTERS, 1980

"His wife wants him to retire, that's for sure," Kaminski said as the squad stood around Maggiotto's desk.

"He's got the time in, I know that," Schoetz said, handing Maggiotto his second cup of coffee that morning.

"Yes, but you guys still have some things to learn," Dunleavy said, taking off his hat as he came into the bullpen area. The homicide detectives all looked up, smiling, and a round of "Good morning Chief," and "Good to see you back, boss" went around the room.

"I see, Rico, that you're third on the list for Lieutenant," Dunleavy said.

"Yeah, but they'd never assign me back to homicide right off the bat, boss."

"Another reason for me to stick around here a while longer. C'mon in my office, Rico, there's something I want to show you," Dunleavy said, pulling the key to the unmarked file drawer out of his pocket.

Acknowledgments.

I would like to thank the following people and organizations for their time, their knowledge, and especially their patience in guiding me through the writing of this book. Any mistakes are entirely my own. Mark Stanbach, Elizabeth Leik , Mary Kokoski, Mike Kaska, Kevin Kinal, Gary Coleman, Zack Lovelace, Norm Effman, D. Greene, the 1030 Tech Support Staff, Bill O'Conner, Lee Coppola, the staff of the Grovesnor Room of the Buffalo and Erie County Public Library, Dave Pfalzgraf, Jan in the Erie County Clerk's Office, Ric Cottom, my brothers at the Buffalo Fire Historical Museum, Bill Keenan, Mary Clare Keenan, John Toolen, Tara Mulligan, Robert Lauro, Tom Angell, Heather Georghiou of the Newburgh Free Library, the Buffalo and Erie County Historical Society, Frank Goderre, Francisco Miranda and Barbara Carey at the Field Library, Peekskill, NY, and the Barone Family for their hospitality and a million laughs through the years.

About the Author.

Mark Hannon is a retired firefighter who grew up in Buffalo, New York. He is also the author of the crime novels *Every Man for Himself* and *The Vultures*; a history, *The Fire Laddies*; and numerous short stories. He and his family make their home in Baltimore, Maryland.

If you enjoyed this book,
please consider writing a review
and sharing it with other readers.

Many of our authors are happy to participate in
Book Club and Reader Group discussions.
For more information, contact us at info@encirclepub.com.

Thank you,
Encircle Publications

For news about more exciting new fiction, join us at:

Facebook: www.facebook.com/encirclepub

Instagram: www.instagram.com/encirclepublications

Sign up for the Encircle Publications newsletter:
eepurl.com/cs8taP

Made in United States
North Haven, CT
12 December 2023

45591247R00171